Deadly Deception

Cruise Ship Chronicles
Cozy Mystery Series Book 4

Hope Callaghan

www.hopecallaghan.com

Copyright © 2015
All rights reserved.

This book is a work of fiction. Although places mentioned may be real, the characters, names and incidents and all other details are products of the author's imagination and are used fictitiously. Any resemblance to actual events or actual persons, living or dead is purely coincidental.

No part of this publication may be copied, reproduced in any format, by any means, electronic or otherwise, without prior consent from the copyright owner and publisher of this book. The only exception is brief quotations in printed reviews.

Visit my website for new releases and special offers: www.HopeCallaghan.com

A special **thank you** to **Peggy Hyndman and Wanda Downs** for taking the time to read and review the fourth book in my series, Cruise Ship Chronicles, *Deadly Deception* and offering all of the helpful advice!

***

Table of Contents

Chapter 1

Chapter 2

Chapter 3

Chapter 4

Chapter 5

Chapter 6

Chapter 7

Chapter 8

Chapter 9

Chapter 10

Chapter 11

Chapter 12

Chapter 13

Chapter 14

Chapter 15

Chapter 16

Chapter 17

Chapter 18

Chapter 19

Chapter 20

Chapter 21

Pumpkin Pecan Cobbler

About The Author

Chapter 1

Millie Sanders smelled trouble from the moment Ariana Teliar stepped on board Siren of the Seas with her massive steamer trunks and personal assistant.

The slender, blonde woman raised a ruckus from the second she crossed over the threshold that led into the atrium. Millie had heard they were getting a "famous" lead entertainer. Earlier that day Andy Walker, Millie's boss, had a pep talk with the staff, telling them that Siren was lucky to have Ariana agree to a weeklong trial run...with stipulations, of course.

Judging by the excessive baggage and personal assistant that stood next to the young woman, Millie had a good idea what those stipulations were.

Andy shook his head and let out a low whistle. Technically, Andy would be Ariana's boss, but

Millie's personal observations told her it might just be the other way around.

Millie, never one to shrink away from a challenge, stepped forward. She thrust her hand toward the perfectly coiffed willowy blonde, who was wearing enough makeup to start her own Mary Kay franchise. "Hello. I'm Millie Sanders, Assistant Cruise Director. Welcome to Siren of the Seas."

Andy stepped beside her. "I'm Andy Walker, Cruise Director." Ariana ignored Millie and shook Andy's hand as she batted her long, fake eyelashes. "How do you do. I am Ariana Teliar." She turned to the woman standing next to her. "This is my personal assistant, Kay."

Kay, a stocky, middle-aged woman with sad eyes and nondescript features, smiled. In that moment, Millie felt sorry for the woman...very sorry.

Andy had asked Millie to show Ariana to her cabin the day they had found out the woman would be joining the staff. At the time, Millie had been a little miffed when she found out Ariana would not be residing in a standard crew cabin, but rather in a suite that was more like efficiency, with a kitchenette, small living area and separate shower with a tub. On top of that, she was on an upper deck and even had a private balcony!

Millie turned to lead Ariana and her assistant across the lobby when a small man with a thick, full moustache stepped from around Ariana's shadow. "Where shall I stay?"

Millie had not noticed the man before.

Ariana waved a dismissive hand. "Oh. Pierre. I almost forgot. Pierre must accompany me, as well."

This was the first that Millie had heard of a third person. It appeared that Ariana now had a complete entourage of two...unless of course there were more people ready to pop up out of nowhere.

Andy frowned. He knew that Ariana had brought an assistant, but a third person...where would they put him? "Let me make a quick call," he mumbled. He turned his back and stepped away.

Ariana sniffed. "I don't know why this is such a big deal. I mean, Pierre can bunk with anyone. Right Pierre?"

Pierre narrowed his eyes and glared at Ariana. "Of course, Ms. Teliar," he gritted through clenched teeth.

If the tone of his voice bothered Ariana Teliar, it didn't show. She ignored his comment and for the first time, acknowledged Millie's presence. "Pierre can stay here while they work out his sleeping arrangements. I need to get settled." She shifted the designer bag on her shoulder and waved her arm at Millie to proceed.

Millie stepped in front of Ariana. "This way."

She didn't wait for an answer as she headed to the bank of elevators. Although Millie hated elevators with a passion, she had sneaky suspicion that Ariana would raise a stink if she had to take the stairs.

Millie jabbed the "down" button with her thumb and waited, praying the elevator on the left, the one that Millie had been stuck in a few months ago, would not be the one that they would have to take.

She watched the glass elevators race each other down to deck five. It appeared that the middle elevator would arrive first but as luck would have it, the one on the left dinged first and the doors silently slid open.

Millie sucked in a breath. "Please let us make it to deck four safe and sound," she whispered under her breath. It was only one floor down. What could possibly happen?

The three women and one of the crew, who trailed behind lugging Ariana's bags, squeezed into the elevator for the short ride. The doors closed, the elevator jolted and then let out a low groan as it slowly descended one floor.

"I think there is too much weight inside this elevator," Joseph, the crewmember, insisted.

Ariana sniffed. "My luggage can't weigh more than I do."

"That's what I mean," Joseph answered. "These suitcases weigh a ton."

Millie covered her mouth to keep from laughing.

Kay, who stood facing Millie, didn't crack a smile. If she appreciated the humor in Joseph's offhand remark, she hid it well.

Thank goodness, the elevator doors finally opened and the women waited while Joseph maneuvered the luggage through the narrow opening and out into the lobby.

Millie stood to the side while Ariana flounced out of the elevator, followed by Kay. "This way." She waved them into the upper level of the main theater and to the right.

Joseph, who trailed behind, paused. "Miss Millie, are you sure we are going the right way?" He was confused and for good reason.

"I'm positive, Joseph," she assured him.

The small group passed the sound booth and lighting area as they made their way along the back of the theater.

The door to the private suite was not marked and, in fact, blended in with the wall. Millie fumbled for the handle. She grasped the flat piece of metal, pulled it forward and at the same time pushed on the door.

The door swung open and light poured out into the dark theater.

Millie stepped into the suite first. She had first learned of its existence the day before when Andy had brought her here.

He had explained that they used the suite for VIP entertainers that were only onboard for a couple days. The entertainers would board in one port. When they finished their scheduled shows, they would disembark at the next port for their flight home. During their time onboard, they stayed in the spacious suite...a suite that Ariana Teliar would now be using.

The woman followed Millie inside. She studied the space with a critical eye as she slowly spun around. Ariana wandered over to the door that opened out onto the balcony and flicked the edge of the curtain with her fingertip. "At least I can get some fresh air," she sniffed.

"Where do I sleep?" Kay, the assistant, had finally found her voice.

"In here." Millie shuffled to a connecting door off to the side. She swung the door open and fumbled for the light switch. The room was much smaller than Ariana's suite but at least she wouldn't have to share.

Inside was a narrow bunk bed, tucked up against the wall and a small dresser with a tiny TV above it. Off in the corner was a bathroom, barely large enough to turn around.

Kay nodded. "This is nice." It was apparent that Kay was used to small confined spaces.

Poor thing, Millie thought. Not only did she have to deal with Ariana, it was obvious she was used to whatever scraps Ariana threw her way.

Joseph tugged the trunks across the threshold and into the room. "Where should I put these Miss Millie?"

"You can stack them over there." She pointed to an open space in the far corner of the room.

Ariana spun around, her face twisted in an ugly scowl. "He can't just leave them," she snapped.

Joseph paused; the deer in the headlight look on his face as he warily glanced from Millie to Ariana.

"He can and he will," Millie said firmly. She nodded to Joseph. "Thank you, Joseph."

Joseph darted out of the room before the sparks started to fly. He knew Millie well enough to know that once she put her foot down, she meant business.

Ariana tapped the tip of her high-heeled shoe on the floor. "Now what am I supposed to do?"

Millie mimicked her pose. "Well, if you don't want to run around in your birthday suit, I suggest you unpack your bags!"

Millie marched out of the cabin and firmly closed the door behind her. *Five days, Millie. You've only got five days,* she told herself.

Millie stomped back to the atrium and Andy, who stood near the ship's entrance.

He grinned when he saw the scowl on Millie's face. "Is she that bad?"

Millie snorted. "Worse...much worse."

They spent the rest of the afternoon greeting the new arrivals and directing them to various areas of the ship. Millie was up to her eyeballs directing passengers and forgot all about Ariana Teliar.

Millie made it backstage only moments before the curtains went up for the beginning of the Welcome Aboard show later that day. Millie peeked behind the velvet curtain to study the crowd. She could tell a lot about the passengers by judging how full the first night's show was. The higher the turnout the first night, the more active the passengers tended to be.

Millie waited until the show had ended and the performers cleared the back before she stopped by Andy's office to go over the next day's schedule.

She squeezed into the chair next to him and glanced at the sheet. Tomorrow was this voyage's first day at sea and one of the busiest days of the week. Millie was excited. The ship had just changed routes and instead of visiting the Bahamas and South Seas Cay, they would be visiting the Western Caribbean and Cozumel, Mexico.

Millie had never been to Cozumel. From what she had heard, it was one of the most popular stops for the crew and she could hardly wait to check it out. She slid her reading glasses on and peered down at the sheet. Millie frowned as she read the big, bold letters at the top of the sheet: *TRAIN ARIANA*.

Millie frowned. "That...that isn't *me* training Ariana, is it?"

Andy dropped the pen he had been holding and began to massage his temple. "I don't have time Millie. I need someone who can handle her with kid gloves. It looks as if she might be high maintenance and I can't think of a better person to keep her in line than you."

"But…"

Andy cut her off. "I'm sorry, Millie. It has to be you." She could tell from the tone of his voice that the decision was final. There was no point in arguing.

"Alright, but I can't be held responsible if her snarky attitude gets her in trouble," she warned.

"I knew I could count on you." Andy patted Millie's arm. "Stop by her cabin on your way down in the morning."

Millie slid the chair back and stood. "I suppose. If you don't need anything else, I'm going to turn in."

Andy waved her off and Millie shuffled out of the theater and headed to her cabin.

Her plan had been to stop by the gift shop and check on her friend, Cat, who had recently received a suspicious envelope from her ex-husband.

She decided to wait until morning and instead, made a beeline for her cabin. She stepped inside the cabin, kicked off her shoes and removed her socks. She slowly walked back and forth on the carpeted floor, wondering how she had managed to be stuck with Ariana.

Millie stripped off her clothes and pulled on her pajamas before she headed to the bathroom to brush her teeth and wash her face. Finally, she slid between the sheets and tucked them under her chin. She folded her hands and closed her eyes. "Dear Lord, please help me survive Ariana Teliar."

***

The next morning, Millie climbed out of bed before the alarm went off. Sarah, Millie's cabin mate, was in the bathroom. Millie waited for her to emerge before she grabbed a clean uniform from the closet and started for the bathroom door.

Sarah reached for her lanyard that hung on the wall hook. "What's with the glum face?" she asked.

"Ariana Teliar," Millie moped.

"Oh!" Sarah frowned. "Have you met her? I heard she's a real trip."

"Not only have I met her, I have to train her," Millie said.

Sarah grimaced. "Good luck with that one."

Sarah headed out of the cabin while Millie disappeared into the small bathroom to get ready. She wondered if Andy had managed to find Pierre, Ariana's other assistant, a place to sleep. Maybe he had to shack up with Andy. The thought of Andy having to share his cabin made her smile.

Millie slipped into her work uniform, smoothed her hair away from her face and clipped it in a messy bun in the back of her head. It was time to start her day and the first thing on her to-do list was track down Ariana!

Millie climbed the steps to the theater and made her way inside. The inside of the theater was dark and it took Millie's eyes a moment to adjust to the lack of light.

She made a quick right and headed toward Ariana's suite. Millie made it about halfway across the room when Ariana flung the door to her suite wide open. "There's a body on my balcony!"

Chapter 2

Millie jogged across the theater and followed Ariana into the suite. Kay was standing near the door that led out to the balcony, her eyes as round as saucers. "She's right. There's someone out there."

Millie peeked over Kay's shoulder and out onto the balcony. At first glance, Millie didn't recognize the male figure, lying on his back with both arms and legs twisted at odd angles.

The man was wearing a security guard uniform and now that she was able to get a good look at his face, she recognized him but couldn't remember his name. He was one of the crew that scanned passengers' belongings when they boarded the ship.

Although Millie was almost 100% certain the man was dead; she placed two fingers on the side of his neck and checked for a pulse. His skin was cold and clammy and her stomach began to churn.

She took a step back. Her eyes never left the body as she plucked her radio from her belt. She lifted it to her lips and pressed the button. "Dave Patterson, do you copy?"

She waited for a brief moment.

"Patterson here. Go ahead, Millie."

It took a split second for Millie to decide she didn't want to announce to the world that a body had been discovered. "I need you to meet me on the upper level of the theater ASAP."

"I'm on my way," was the clipped response.

She glanced at Ariana's assistant, Kay. "Can you please meet Mr. Patterson by the entrance?"

Kay nodded and headed out the door.

The severity of the situation and the fact that there was a dead man on her balcony finally sank in and Ariana began to sway. She lifted a hand to her brow. "I-I'm dizzy."

Millie watched as Ariana rocked back and forth in slow motion. Millie, skeptical that this was all an act...a ploy for attention, gave her a 50/50 chance of actually passing out.

Instead of collapsing, Ariana reached for the chair behind her and slumped backward onto the seat. Her eyes fluttered shut.

Patterson strode through the open door. "You found a body?"

Millie shook her head. "Not me." She pointed to Ariana. "She did. He's out on the balcony."

Patterson stepped out onto the balcony and leaned over the lifeless body. "Miguel."

Patterson unclipped his radio from his belt and then changed his mind. "I better not do that."

Millie had to agree. It was probably best not to announce Miguel's death for all to hear.

He stepped into the suite and headed for the phone that hung on the wall above the small desk area. He jabbed the buttons on the number pad and waited for someone on the other end to pick up. "I need Doctor Gundervan, two security guards, a stretcher and a cover...stat! Have them meet me outside the upper level of the main theater."

He silently listened for a moment before dropping the handset in the cradle.

Kay cowered in the corner while Ariana began to whimper. "Oh...I feel sick," she moaned. No one made a move to help...not even Kay.

While Patterson made his way into the hall to wait for Doctor Gundervan and security, Millie reached inside her pocket and pulled her cellphone out.

She turned it to camera mode and stepped out onto the balcony where she snapped a few quick pictures of Miguel's body. She took several photos of the balcony itself and then started to take a few of the inside of the suite.

"What are you doing?" Ariana hissed, her nausea forgotten.

"This is a crime scene," Millie explained.

"Maybe he snuck out onto my balcony and had a heart attack or something," Ariana guessed.

Millie shook her head. "Judging by the marks around his neck, I would say he was strangled."

Patterson, along with Doctor Gundervan and the security guards, stepped into the room.

While Gundervan headed to the balcony to examine the body, Patterson stayed inside to ask Ariana and Kay several questions. He pulled a notepad from his pocket and grabbed a pen from the top of the desk. "Which one of you discovered the body?"

Ariana and Kay each pointed at the other. "Her."

Ariana crossed her arms. "I did not," she insisted.

Kay rolled her eyes, as if to dispute Ariana's statement.

Patterson looked up. "You both found the body."

He went on. "Did you notice anyone lurking around outside the door?"

Both were able to agree on that point and shook their heads "no."

Patterson asked them when the body was found and the two women gave him conflicting times. He finally gave up on getting a straight answer, flipped the pad shut and shoved it in his pocket. "That's all for now. I'll let you know if I have any other questions. I need you to step out into the hall."

Kay reached for Ariana's hand and the two of them shuffled out of the room.

Patterson nodded at Millie. "You, too." He lowered his voice. "I need you to listen in on their conversation."

Millie raised a brow. She hadn't thought about that! Right now, it looked as if Kay and Ariana were the prime suspects. After all, there was only one way to get to the balcony, which was through the main door and both women had keys to the suite.

She found the women hovering near a row of theater seats. Kay stood over Ariana and fanned her face while Ariana wept, although Millie noticed there were no tears. "My lips are parched," she moaned as she eyed Millie.

If this was Ariana's attempt to get rid of Millie, it wasn't going to work. "We need to stay here until Patterson tells us we're free to leave."

"Why? What's going on?" Millie turned to see Pierre, Ariana's other assistant, make his way over.

Ariana jerked forward in her chair and clawed at Pierre's arm. "Pierre! There's a dead man on my balcony!"

Pierre turned to Kay, who confirmed the statement with a nod of her head. "It's true."

Pierre dropped to his knees and rubbed Ariana's hand. "Oh, my. Are you okay?"

Ariana shuddered. "Every time I close my eyes, I see that poor man's body."

Pierre continued to fawn over Ariana, which made Millie want to throw up. The woman was as artificial as her eyelashes.

They waited for a good hour before the guards and the stretcher, carrying the body, passed by on its way out of the theater. It wasn't a moment too soon. Millie had heard just about enough of Ariana's moaning and groaning to last a lifetime.

A movement caught Millie's eye and she watched a dark figure climb the side steps to the upper level. It was Andy. "Zack just told me there was some sort of commotion up here. What's going on?"

"We found a dead man on my balcony," Ariana replied, her voice rising shrilly. "What kind of cabin did you give me?"

Andy ignored Ariana. He turned to Millie. "What happened?"

Millie briefly explained all that she knew – which wasn't much. "Patterson and the detectives just left," she finished.

"So it's safe to go back inside?" he asked. He didn't wait for a reply. Instead, he headed to the cabin. Millie was right behind him. She hoped that Ariana and her entourage would stay put.

"She's driving me crazy," Millie told Andy when they were out of earshot.

Andy shot her a sideways glance. "I'm sorry, Millie. I don't know what else to do with her and I don't trust anyone but you."

He glanced out toward the balcony. "You don't think she was the target and the killer made a mistake?"

Millie followed him out onto the balcony and glanced around. The space was private, unlike the passenger balconies where if you leaned forward and tilted your head, you could peek around the side and see directly into your neighbor's balcony.

Millie hadn't previously noticed the small, half door, which was part of the wall that separated the balcony. Millie pointed. "Where does that lead?"

"I'm not sure," Andy admitted. He fished inside his pocket and pulled out a small ring of keys. "Let me see if one of my master keys fits the lock."

He shoved the key in the lock and turned. The lock wouldn't budge. He pulled the key back out and studied the notches. "Whoops! Wrong one."

He flipped through the ring and tried a second key. It fit perfectly and the door popped open.

Millie knelt down and peered through the opening. It was some sort of catwalk that ran along the side of the ship. On the other end was another door, identical to the one Millie was looking through. "I wonder what's on the other side of that door."

She grabbed the handrail and pulled herself to her feet. "Miguel had to have come in through the cabin door or across this small catwalk."

Millie had a sneaky suspicion that Andy had been withholding information. She nodded toward the door. "Ariana. What's her story?"

A muscle in Andy's jaw began to twitch. "I didn't want to get into all that, but I guess I'll have to."

Andy went on to explain that Ariana was Ariana Gatwick, heir to a real estate empire.

The young woman had recently received several death threats. Whoever was out to get her had gone as far as to break into the family compound and murder Ms. Gatwick's assistant, mistaking the poor woman for Ariana.

Ariana's father, in a panic to protect his daughter, decided to get her out of the country and called on his close friend, Ted Danvers, CEO of Majestic Cruise Lines, to arrange for his daughter to board the ship as a temporary employee, Ariana Teliar.

"You're telling me that we're responsible for this woman's safety and someone is out to kill her?" Millie felt sorry for Ariana – but that didn't make her like her any better. She was still a pain in the rear.

Andy sighed. "It appears so. Now that a body was found on her balcony, that means the killer must have followed her here."

"What about her staff? Maybe one of them is out to get her?" It wouldn't be far off. Millie could see how the woman could push someone right over the edge.

Andy shrugged. "We were told Pierre and Kay had already been screened and posed no threat."

Millie ran her hand lightly along the rail. "That means that there is someone else, a hitman disguised as another passenger, onboard and within striking distance."

"It appears so," he admitted. "Because of that, you're going to have to stick even closer to Ariana."

"Why not a security guard?" Millie wondered aloud.

"We have guards watching, as well," Andy told her. "For liability purposes, we need a woman. We need you."

Millie gazed out at the open water. She turned to face Andy. "I guess I can keep an eye on her,"

Millie relented. "As long as I don't have to stay with her night and day."

Andy grimly shook his head. "I'm afraid it will be 24/7. Housekeeping is on their way to deliver a cot to her room," Andy said.

Millie crossed her arms. "Oh no you don't. That woman makes me want to rip my hair out of my head. Why, I'll go stark raving mad!"

"Don't be so dramatic," Andy teased.

"See? She's already rubbing off on me," Millie groaned.

"You'll get double pay," Andy tempted.

Millie paused. Double pay. She could use the extra money to buy a plane ticket home for her upcoming break, which was right after the holidays...

Millie's eyes narrowed. "How long?"

Andy could see she was starting to cave. "Only for this week," he reassured her.

"So I only have to babysit until the ship docks in Miami?"

He nodded. "Yes. Millie, you're the only one I trust. We can't have a male guard her. We need a female. You're the closest thing we've got."

"What if I were to...track down the killer before the week is up, then what?" she asked.

"Then you're off the hook. You can go back to life as normal."

Millie mulled it over. On the one hand, she could use the extra money. If she could figure out who was trying to take Ariana out, she could have her life back. On top of that, it was only for a week. How bad could it be?

She stuck her hand out. "It's a deal."

Chapter 3

Millie left Andy to explain the situation to Ariana and Kay while she headed upstairs to talk to her friends, Annette Delacroix and Cat Wellington. Maybe the three of them could put their heads together and come up with a plan to flush out the killer.

Millie was in luck. Annette, who worked in the kitchen, had just gone on break. Millie and she headed to the gift shop to track down Cat.

It was still early and the gift shop where Cat worked was like a ghost town. Millie briefly explained to the girls what had transpired since Ariana had boarded and how she was now her "roommate" for the duration of the trip.

"So I need to flush out the stalker/killer before he...or she strikes again," she finished.

Annette tapped the side of her cheek. "Seems to me the most logical suspects would be her assistants."

Millie nodded. "I've already thought about that. They have both been cleared."

Cat adjusted her beehive hairdo. "Miguel worked the scanners. Could it be the killer had tried to go through security with a weapon and when Miguel confronted him, he killed him?"

"Good point," Millie said. It was true. Someone had wanted Miguel out of the picture...just like they would want Millie out of the picture. She made a mental note to pack her stun gun/flashlight in her bag before she headed to Ariana's suite.

Cat wrinkled her nose. "I don't envy you. Rumor has it this woman is a real diva."

"She is," Millie agreed. "At least it's only for a week." She turned to face the girls. "If I can figure out who is out to get her, I'm off the hook."

Annette glanced at her watch. "I've got to get back to work." She stood. "You need to find out more about this woman and her staff so we know what we're up against."

Millie groaned. "I know. I'm heading back up there now." She followed Annette to the door. "Pray for me," she pleaded. "I'm going to need it."

***

"I have a very strict schedule. Awake at 7:00 a.m. for yoga, followed by an organic vegetable smoothie and fat-free yogurt breakfast. After that, I like to read my fan mail."

The woman actually has fans? Millie rolled her eyes.

Ariana appeared not to notice and continued her recital.

"At ten, I have an hour catnap; followed by a visit to the spa to make sure my hair and nails are in tip top condition. After the spa, I eat a light lunch, usually a tossed salad with vinaigrette dressing and then free time."

Millie set her pen down. She'd been jotting down notes of Ariana's daily routine and wondered what "free time" entailed.

Ariana continued to pace the floor. "At 1:00, I begin practice which lasts for two hours, followed by a long walk to stretch my limbs. I like to eat dinner early, around 4:30, followed by another hour of practice. The rest of the evening is spent on stage."

The schedule was one Millie hoped she could work with. She glanced at Kay, who looked bored out of her mind.

Ariana snapped her fingers. "Oh! Of course, Kay helps with my stage costume and makeup before the show."

Millie, who sat on the cot the maintenance crew had dropped off, tried to shift to a more comfortable position. The cot was harder than a rock and Millie was convinced she was going to have some rough nights ahead.

Millie studied the woman out of the corner of her eye. She looked much younger without the thick layer of makeup she'd had on the day before. She was quite attractive.

Millie wondered if maybe there was a scorned ex or jealous woman who had a score to even.

"Who do you think wants to cause you harm?" Millie asked point blank.

Ariana stopped pacing and frowned. "Why, I can't imagine anyone wanting to harm me."

Kay snorted.

Millie had to agree with the snort.

"Jilted ex? Scorned lover?" Millie probed.

Ariana lifted her nail to inspect it. "Well, I suppose..."

"Have you ever received death threats before just recently? A note or text?"

Ariana shook her head. "No. Never."

Millie raised a brow.

"I swear," she insisted. "It just started happening."

There was a knock on the door, which interrupted Millie's interrogation. Ariana and Kay didn't make a move to answer to door.

Millie shifted to the side as she struggled to get off the cot. When she got to the door, she peeked through the peephole before she opened it. It was Pierre.

She swung the door open and stepped aside. He squeezed past her, carrying several long gowns.

Ariana eyed the gowns. "I told you to hang onto those."

"There's no room in the cabin. They are getting wrinkled," he explained.

Ariana rushed forward and reached for a dress. "Oh no! Why didn't tell me that?"

Millie stared at her shoes and counted to ten.

She focused her attention on Pierre. He was a man of few words, not that he could get a word in edgewise when Ariana was around anyway!

"Pierre, do you have any idea who might want to harm Ariana?"

Pierre handed the last gown to Kay and shook his head. "No, I don't."

"See?" Ariana snapped. "It's probably just some random psycho."

"What about kidnap and hold for ransom?"

Kay nodded. "That's what I thought, until that poor man was found on the balcony yesterday."

"What about Ariana's former assistant?" Millie asked. She remembered Andy telling her someone had murdered the woman.

Ariana shrugged. "This conversation is going nowhere." She changed the subject as she talked to Pierre and Kay about the rest of her costumes.

Millie glanced at her watch. It was time to pick up Scout, Captain Armati's dog. She hadn't seen him in a couple days and knew he'd be anxious to get out of the apartment. "I'll be back shortly."

The trio acted as if she was now invisible and didn't even look up when she headed for the door.

Millie closed the door behind her. Just being out of the room brightened Millie's spirits and with a spring in her step, she headed to the bridge.

On the way to the bridge, Millie mulled over what little she knew. Kidnapping was a great theory, but it was apparent that whoever was after Ariana had no qualms about killing.

The thought persisted in the back of her mind that Miguel had been onto something and that was why someone had murdered him. She still couldn't rule out Kay or Pierre. Perhaps if she could get her hands on a copy of the passenger list – the manifest – she could check the list to see if anyone else looked suspicious.

Millie tapped on the outside bridge door and then let herself in using her keycard. Captain Armati wasn't in the room, but Captain Vitale was.

Millie smiled. It was nice to see Captain Vitale, who had recently returned to the ship after being poisoned. "Good morning, Millie."

"Good morning, Captain Vitale. Is Captain Armati around?"

Vitale shook his head. "I believe he's down in Patterson's office."

Millie nodded. Patterson was probably filling the captain in on poor Miguel's demise.

She wandered down the small hall to the captain's private quarters. Captain Armati had given Millie the door code to let herself in when he wasn't around.

She punched in the code, waited for the beep and then pushed the door open.

Scout, the captain's teacup Yorkie, met her at the door. She dropped to her knees and waited while Scout climbed onto her legs. He pawed the front of her blouse and when she leaned down, he licked the side of her face and then bit her chin.

"I guess you're happy to see me," she laughed.

Scout hopped off her lap and then pranced around her in circles. "Woof!"

Millie led Scout out onto the balcony so that he could use his potty pad before they headed out. She locked the slider door and then wandered to the front. When he was done, she tucked him in the crook of her arm and then grabbed his carrier.

When she opened the door, she came face-to-face with the captain. "Hello Millie."

Millie turned a light shade of pink. "Hello N-, Captain Armati," she corrected herself. She reminded herself she could only call the captain "Nic" when they were alone...

"I just left Dave Patterson's office. It seems we have a sticky situation on our hands with Ms. Teliar."

Millie nodded. "It would appear so."

The captain tucked his arms behind his back and studied her face. "I appreciate your offer to keep an eye on Ms. Teliar while she's in our care."

"I'm not sure it was an offer." Millie chuckled. "More like Andy strong armed me!"

The captain nodded. "Ah, but you are loyal to Andy and I appreciate your willingness to pitch in and help."

"You're welcome." She glanced down at Scout who started to wiggle free. "I hope she likes dogs."

The captain walked Scout and Millie to the outer door that connected the bridge to the hall. He held the door open and waited for Scout and Millie to step into the hall. "I shall see you two later."

He closed the door behind them and Millie started down the steps. She glanced down at her watch. It was already close to 11:00 and she wondered if Ariana was at the spa.

She decided to check the suite first and tapped on Ariana's door. Kay opened the door and peeked through the crack. When she saw Millie, she swung the door open. "Ariana went up to the spa."

Kay suddenly noticed Scout. She stuck her palm out for Scout to inspect. "Oh, what a cute dog!"

"Scout," Millie said.

"Scout. Can I hold him?"

Millie handed Scout to Kay and she snuggled him against her chest. "I used to have a teacup Yorkie when I was young. Her name was Pippy and she was a stinker."

Kay held the dog so they were eye level. "I bet you're a stinker, too."

Scout licked her cheek and she laughed as she handed Scout back.

"How long have you known Ariana?" Millie asked.

"Not long," Kay said. "Although we once lived in the same neighborhood."

Millie frowned. Ariana's family was wealthy, according to Andy. Why would a woman who came from money want to work as an assistant to Ariana?

Kay answered, as if she had read Millie's mind. "My family fell on hard times when the stock market crashed. I had to find a job and after Ariana's other assistant...err...passed, Ariana was looking for a replacement," she explained. "Ariana is...difficult, but the pay is good and the fringe benefits even better."

"So you will get to travel with this job?"

Kay nodded. "Yeah, and once you get used to Ariana, she's okay."

"What about Pierre? Do you know how long he's known Ariana?"

Kay shook her head. "Nope. Pierre is a man of few words. Getting him to talk is like pulling teeth."

"Did you notice any odd noises or sounds last night or early this morning?" Millie continued.

"You mean like outside on the balcony? No, but then I'm a sound sleeper. Not much wakes me up," Kay admitted.

Millie shifted Scout and the bag. "I guess I better track Ariana down since I am now her unofficial bodyguard."

"Yeah," Kay smirked. "See ya' later."

Millie and Scout headed out of the theater and started up the stairs to the spa, which was several floors up and directly above the theater.

When they reached the spa deck, Millie set Scout on the floor and snapped the leash to his collar.

He darted down the hall and Millie had to power-walk just to keep up with him.

Millie opened the glass door leading into the spa and waited while Scout trotted ahead of her. She nodded to the girl behind the counter whose name she could never remember.

She squinted to read the tag. *Jade*.

"I'm looking for..."

Jade nodded. "Ms. Ariana." She pointed to the side entrance. "She's in there."

"Thank you."

Scout and Millie wandered into the back room and found Ariana seated in one of the leather lounge chairs, her feet propped up on a stool. "...with just a hint of fuschia on the tips," she told the girl.

She looked up when she saw Millie. "Oh! There you are. I tried to wait for you back in the room but when you never showed up, I decided to take matters into my own hands. You need to do a better job of time management," she scolded Millie.

Millie opened her mouth to let her have it and promptly closed it. *Five days, Millie. You have just five days. Think of all that extra money that will pay for the plane ticket home.*

She gritted her teeth and smiled. "I had to pick up Scout."

Ariana flinched and lowered her gaze. "You brought a dog? They allow dogs onboard? He- he's not staying with us..."

As much as Millie would have loved to tell Ariana the dog *would* be staying with them, just to get her goat, she shook her head. "No. Scout is Captain Armati's dog. I keep him during the day and then take him home in the evening," she explained.

Ariana was visibly relieved. "Good. Dogs have germs and rabies."

Millie and Scout hung around a few more minutes as they waited for the spa employee to finish Ariana's pedicure.

After she finished, the women walked back to Ariana's suite.

Ariana used her key card to unlock the door and then pushed the door open. The room was empty. Kay was nowhere in sight.

Millie set Scout on the floor and headed for the adjoining door that connected Ariana and Kay's cabin.

Millie tapped on the outer door. There was no answer so Millie turned the door handle and stepped inside the windowless room. The small space was pitch dark and she was afraid to flip the light switch, just in case Kay was napping.

She quietly closed the door behind her while Scout circled her feet.

Ariana's perfectly manicured fingertips flew to her throat. "You-you're not going to let that creature roam freely in my room?"

That was exactly what Millie planned to do.

Ariana hovered behind the small desk chair and used the chair as a barricade to keep Scout at bay. She wasn't kidding when she said she didn't like dogs.

Scout was on his best behavior. When he trotted around the side of the chair to say hello, Ariana nudged him with her foot, which angered Millie. It was bad enough that she had to take the woman's abuse. There was no way she would subject poor Scout to the same treatment.

She promptly picked Scout up and cradled him in her arms. "I'll be back shortly," she said stiffly.

"Alone, I hope," Ariana retorted.

"Alone." Millie strode over to the door and let herself out, yanking it shut behind her with one swift pull.

"I swear that woman is going to push me right over the edge," Millie muttered.

Chapter 4

Back inside the bridge, Millie explained to Captain Armati, Ariana's aversion to dogs and although he was sad for Scout and Millie, he told her that he understood.

"As soon as I don't have to babysit that woman anymore, I'll be back." Millie blinked back tears as she handed Scout to the captain.

She trudged back to Ariana's suite, her feet dragging on the floor, as if she were heading to her own execution. She tapped on the outside cabin door and sucked in a breath. "Patience, Lord. Please give me patience."

Kay opened the door this time and Millie stepped inside. "She's not here," Kay announced.

Millie frowned. The two women were like musical chairs. First one was gone, then the other. It was almost as if they couldn't stand to be around one another!

"Where did she wander off to now?"

Kay shrugged. "This is the second time she has disappeared." She thrust a note in Millie's hand. "I found this."

Millie unfolded the note. She slipped her reading glasses on.

On the back of a room service order form were the hastily scrawled words: "I'll be back later. Don't bother looking for me."

Millie crumpled the note and tossed it in the trash. "She knows I'm trying to protect her, yet she is bent on making my job harder!" She clenched her fists and stiffened her arms.

Kay shook her head. "She's a handful, I'll give you that."

Millie shoved her reading glasses into her pocket. "Any idea where she might have run off to?"

"Nope. She's been acting kind of weird ever since we boarded, like she's trying to hide something."

"Maybe she's with Pierre?" Millie could start there.

"You can try, but I doubt it." Kay lowered her voice, although there was no one else in the room. "She hates Pierre."

"But why…"

Kay cut her off. "Mr. Teliar hired him, not Ariana."

No wonder Ariana was so bullheaded. Ariana obviously resented the fact that her father ran the show, telling Ariana where she could and could not go and hiring the people that surrounded her. This included Millie, in a roundabout way. Although Ariana was annoying as all get out, Millie was starting to understand her attitude, to a degree.

"What about you, Kay? Did Mr. Teliar hire you, too?"

Kay's eyes dropped to the floor. She nodded and then met Millie's gaze. "But she likes me," she insisted. "I'm sorry she got away," she added.

Millie patted her arm. "Don't worry about it. I'll track her down."

Kay followed her to the door. "Do you want me to help?"

"No. Stay here in case she comes back. If she does, call Guest Services and they can page me on the radio to let me know she has been found."

Kay gave her a small salute. "Yes, ma'am."

Outside the cabin door, Millie paused. Ariana had already visited the spa so she could cross that off the list.

Millie headed to the stairs and the upper decks. She might as well start at the top and work her way down.

By the time Millie hit the last passenger area and there was still no sign of Ariana, her blood began to boil. She was on a wild goose chase and she had visions of Ariana smiling smugly, fully aware that Millie was searching every nook and cranny of the ship.

When she reached deck seven, she made a pit stop in the kitchen. She found her friend, Annette, bent over a large mixing bowl.

Millie wandered over to the counter and peered inside. "Whatcha making?"

"Sage and onion stuffing for the oven roasted turkey." Annette grabbed a clean spoon off the counter, scooped a heaping spoon of moist stuffing and handed it to Millie. "Tell me what you think."

Millie popped the tasty morsel in her mouth. It was delicious – like a taste of Thanksgiving. "Perfect."

"You don't think it needs more salt?"

"Nope." Millie grabbed a paper napkin and dabbed the corners of her lips.

Annette continued to stir. "Where's Scout?" Scout spent most ship days with Millie until early evening when she took him back home.

Millie shook her head. "Ariana despises dogs so I had to take Scout back to the bridge."

"How's that going?"

Millie crossed her arms. "Ariana is MIA, so if you happen to see a platinum blonde, about this tall," Millie lifted her hand a few inches above her head, "I would appreciate a call."

Annette grinned. "I doubt she'll come back here in the kitchen, but if I do see her, I'll be sure to let you know."

"Thanks." Millie glanced up at the wall clock. "I better keep looking."

She waved good-bye and headed out the side door on her way to the gift shop. Maybe Cat had seen her. The gift shop was the perfect location for people watching.

There were several shoppers inside the store, none of whom was Ariana Teliar. She stepped over to the counter and waited while Cat rang up a shopper's purchase.

After the customer left, Cat turned to Millie. "What happened to Scout?"

Millie let out a sigh. "It's a long story." She changed the subject. "You wouldn't have happened to notice a tall, willowy blonde around here, looking like she owned the place..."

Cat scrunched up her nose. "You lost her already?"

"Yeah," Millie admitted. "She gave me the slip."

Cat tucked a wayward strand of hair behind her ear. "Not that I recall but now that I know you're looking for her, I'll be sure to keep an eye out."

If it was any consolation, Millie knew that Ariana would return in time to get ready for her evening performance.

Millie decided to track down Pierre. Now that she thought about it, she didn't know Pierre's last name – or Kay's last name, either. She plucked her radio from her belt and pressed the button. "Andy, do you copy?"

Static. Finally, "Go ahead, Millie."

"I'm trying to track down Pierre, Ariana's assistant. Where is he staying?"

There was a long pause. "I put him in with Zack. EC-149." EC stood for employee cabin, 149 was the cabin number.

"10-4. Thanks."

Millie started to replace the radio but Andy continued to talk. "Why? Is Ariana looking for him?"

Millie had hoped she wouldn't have to tell Andy that she lost Ariana. "Not really," she answered vaguely.

"Let me guess. *You're* looking for Ariana."

Millie sighed. "Yeah. It's a long story, but I had to take Scout back to the bridge and when I returned, she was gone."

The tone of Andy's voice rose a decibel. "Millie..."

"I know, I know. Don't worry, I'll find her." *In one piece and still alive, I hope,* she added silently.

Millie turned the button to lower the volume. She was already stressed out enough about the situation without having Andy add to her grief.

Millie made a beeline for EC-149. The employee corridor was empty and she paused for just a second, her ear to the door before she lifted her hand and rapped lightly. Nothing.

She knocked a second time, but harder. The door swung open and Pierre looked out, his expression grim. When he saw Millie, his face brightened. "Ah, Miss Millie. How can I help you?"

Millie glanced over his shoulder. "I'm looking for Ariana. I hoped that she was with you."

Pierre's black moustache twitched. "No. I have not seen her since I dropped the dresses off earlier. She is missing?"

Millie shifted on her feet. "You could say that."

"Sounds like Ariana." He started to close the door, then pulled it back open. "If I see her, I'll be sure to let you know."

Millie placed the palm of her hand on the door and pressed, catching it just before it closed in her face. "I was just thinking, Pierre, that I never caught your last name."

"Then we are even since I don't know yours," he replied.

"Sanders," she told him. "Millie Sanders."

"Ah. Millie Sanders. It is a nice, strong German name."

"Irish," Millie corrected.

"I won't hold that against you," Pierre joked. "See you later?"

Millie opened her mouth to speak, but Pierre had already closed the door...and Millie still didn't know his last name!

Chapter 5

When Millie returned to Ariana's suite, the first thing she noticed was that the door was ajar. She tilted her head and pressed her ear against the crack. The muffled sound of a television echoed through the opening.

Millie pushed on the door and peeked around the corner. From where she stood, she could see the balcony door was open and the back of someone's head...Ariana's head.

Millie crossed the room and stepped out on to the balcony. "Where have you been? I've been looking all over for you."

Ariana whirled around, the corners of her lips lifted in an impish grin. "Stop being such a worry wart. See? I'm fine?"

Millie crossed her arms and leaned forward. "I'm supposed to keep an eye on you. Where were you?"

Ariana waved an arm in the air. "Exploring the ship. I got bored waiting for you to come back so I went out on my own."

Millie wagged a finger. "You're not supposed to do that. Your antics could get me fired!"

That was a stretch. Millie knew Andy wouldn't fire her for losing track of Ariana. Now if she lost Ariana and the woman ended up dead, that might be a different story!

She involuntarily shuddered at the thought. "If you pull one more stunt like that, I'll borrow a pair of handcuffs from security and handcuff us together."

Ariana opened her mouth to reply, but was stopped short when Kay stepped out onto the balcony. "You're back! You gave Millie and me a bad scare," she scolded. "Where were you?"

"Don't bother," Millie shook her head. "She isn't going to tell us."

Millie put her foot down. "I'm dead serious about the handcuffs, Ariana. Promise me you won't do that again."

"Whatever. I promise," Ariana answered in the most insincere voice Millie had ever heard.

She yawned and glanced down at her watch. "I need to practice, not stand around here arguing about what I do in my free time...what little I have."

Millie had almost forgotten that Ariana was the headliner for the evening. The three women exited the cabin. Millie was the last to leave. She pulled on the door handle, checking to make sure it locked behind her.

For the next couple of hours, Kay and she watched Ariana practice on stage. Millie had to admit that the young woman had talent and an incredible voice.

When she had finished her run through, Ariana wandered down the side steps and over to where Kay and Millie sat. "That worked up my appetite. I'm famished."

Millie was hungry, too. She'd been so obsessed with finding her wayward charge, she had missed lunch. Her stomach grumbled.

Millie figured there was no way Ariana would eat in the crew mess so she opted for the Waves buffet area. Even at that, Ariana started to turn up her nose but Millie nipped that in the bud. "The dining room is closed until 5:45 p.m. If you don't eat here, you don't eat," she pointed out.

Ariana wrinkled her nose and glanced around at the buffet stations. Her gaze settled on the pizza counter. "I suppose I could try the pizza," she sniffed.

Millie led the way and the three women headed to the pizza station. Ariana ordered a slice of pepperoni, a slice of margherita and a deluxe. Millie was hungry, too, but not that hungry. She grabbed a slice of pepperoni and a small Caesar salad.

Kay stopped next door at the deli station for a turkey on country roll, which made Millie's mouth water. She stared down at the pizza on her plate. It was too late to change her mind.

The women headed through the sliding doors to the open air dining and a bistro table off in the corner. Millie set her tray on the table. "I'll grab some lemonade." She headed back inside while the other two rearranged the plates on the small table.

Millie plucked three plastic drink cups from the stack, filled them with ice, topped it with lemonade and returned in time to see Ariana pick up a second slice of pizza. For a woman that was stick thin, she sure could put away some food.

Kay, the complete opposite, was on the plump side. She ate about half her sandwich and left the rest on her plate.

When they finished eating, the women returned to the cabin. Pierre was inside waiting to help Ariana with her wardrobe and makeup.

Millie seized her opportunity for a break and excused herself while Pierre and Kay fussed over Ariana.

She was so excited to have a few free minutes to herself, she wasn't sure what to do first. Finally, she decided the right thing to do was to check in with Andy and to let him know that Ariana had returned and assure him she would not let the woman wander the ship unsupervised!

She found Andy in the dressing room, behind the stage. He was in the middle of a meeting with the other dancers. "I understand that Ms. Teliar is a pain in the rear, but my hands are tied. Can't you see we're all suffering here?"

Millie came up behind him. "Mostly me."

Andy whirled around. "True! At least you're not poor Millie who is saddled with Ariana until this voyage ends."

Alison, one of the dancers, shook the piece of paper she was holding in her hand. "This list of demands is ridiculous and I, for one, refuse to go along with this crock of bull!"

Millie couldn't resist. "What's on the list?" she asked.

"What's on the list? I'll tell you what's on the list!" Alison growled. "One. All staff must immediately exit the dressing room area when I arrive."

"Two. Fresh flowers, preferably purple hyacinths, must be arranged in a glass vase and sitting to the left of my dressing room mirror."

"Three and this one is my favorite," Alison spat out. "At all times, I shall lead staff onto the stage and be the first to exit the stage."

Alison's face became a mask of unbridled fury. "Here's what I think of this baloney!" She lifted the sheet of paper, ripped it in half and crumpled both pieces in her hand. She tossed them on the floor and began to stomp on them. Millie could only imagine Alison pretending it was Ariana's face.

Millie had never seen Alison, who was normally calm, serene and sweet, so angry. She almost felt sorry for Ariana.

Unfortunately, Ariana's timing was horrible and she walked in while Alison was grinding the offensive list with the bottom of her shoe.

Ariana gave Alison a haughty stare and swept by her on her way to the changing area.

Alison started after her. Millie grabbed her arm and shook her head. "She's not worth it," Millie whispered in her ear. "C'mon."

She nudged Alison out of the dressing room and the two of them headed off the stage. "Let's go for a walk. A little fresh air will work wonders."

Alison sucked in a deep breath. "Okay." The women wandered out onto the promenade deck and walked along the rail. By the time they made their second round, Alison was much calmer. "Thanks, Millie. That helped."

Millie patted her arm. "You're welcome." They paused to take in the glorious hues of pink and blue that filled the skies as the sun began to set. "You know, I think Ariana is unhappy."

Alison grabbed the railing with both hands and leaned back. "How could she possibly be unhappy? She has people at her beck and call, she has money, power..."

Millie slowly turned and rested her elbows on the rail thoughtfully. "What about friends? Do you think she has friends?"

Alison snorted. "I doubt it." Her shoulders slumped. "I don't know why it made me so angry. I guess it's just that we work hard as a team, and to have someone like her strut in here and assume she can get whatever she wants ticked me off."

"Why don't you try befriending her?" Millie said. "It makes you the bigger person and maybe, just maybe, she needs a friend."

Millie was not only trying to convince Alison, she was talking to herself. "I think I'll give it a go myself."

She glanced down at her watch. "C'mon. We need to get back inside."

The girls wandered to the upper deck and started to pass by Ariana's suite when Millie noticed the door was ajar. "Hang on a sec," she told Alison.

She stepped over to the door and grabbed the handle. She pushed the door open and glanced inside the room.

Millie's hand flew to her lips as her eyes darted around the room. "Oh my goodness!" The place was in shambles and Kay lay in a crumpled heap in the center of the floor.

***

Millie rushed across the room and knelt down next to Kay. She reached out and touched her wrist. At least she had a pulse!

Alison followed Millie inside. "Is she okay?"

Millie glanced back. "I think so." She plucked her radio from her hip and turned the volume up. "Doctor Gundervan, do you copy?"

"I'm here, Millie."

"I need you at the theater suite please," she said.

"On my way," he answered.

Millie could hear the faint strains of the orchestra as they started to play. "You better get backstage," Millie told Alison.

"Are you sure?" Alison surveyed the trashed room and glanced at the poor woman sprawled out on the floor.

"It's okay," Millie assured her.

Alison took one last glance behind her and then headed backstage.

Millie's eyes darted nervously around the room as she waited for Doctor Gundervan.

Dave Patterson, head of security arrived first. He quickly assessed the situation then dropped next to Millie. Kay appeared to be unconscious but was starting to stir. "What happened?"

"I noticed the door ajar when Alison, one of the dancers, and I were passing by. I opened the door to peek inside and this is what I found."

Gundervan arrived and Millie and Patterson stood back while he kneeled over Kay's still form. "She has a bump on her head. Her vitals are good."

Kay moaned and her eyes fluttered. "Oh..." She tried to sit up, but Gundervan told her to hold still.

"Don't try to move yet." Gundervan spoke in a low voice.

Kay lifted a hand to her forehead. "My head is throbbing." Millie, certain that Kay would be all right, began to survey the room. She wondered what the intruder had been looking for.

Kay lay on the floor for several long moments. "When you're ready, we can head down to the medical center for a more thorough examination," Doctor Gundervan told her.

Millie took a step closer. "How did this happen?"

Kay propped herself on her elbows and squinted her eyes. "Well...someone was at the door and when I opened it, this heavyset man with dark, beady eyes was standing outside. Next thing I know, I'm here on the floor and he was standing over me." She pointed to Gundervan.

Doctor Gundervan helped Kay to her feet. They slowly exited the suite and headed for medical.

By the time Patterson and the other security finished their investigation of the area, Ariana and Andy appeared.

Ariana stepped inside the suite first. She stopped in the doorway and pressed her hands to both cheeks. "What in the world?"

Andy nudged her forward as he tried to look inside. "What happened?"

Patterson shoved his hands in his pockets. "Someone knocked Kay, Ariana's assistant, on the head and then ransacked the suite. My guess is the intruder was looking for something."

He turned to Ariana. "Do you have any idea what the person was searching for?"

"Why...no. None whatsoever. Did they destroy anything?"

Millie frowned. Ariana wasn't concerned about poor Kay. Instead, she was worried about her possessions!

"Aren't you going to ask about Kay?"

Ariana pressed a hand to her forehead. "Yes! Of course. How is Kay?"

"She has a nasty lump on her head and is down in the medical center getting checked out."

Ariana half-listened as she picked up a pile of clothes that had been dumped on the floor.

Millie stepped closer. "Don't you want to check on her?"

Ariana glanced up. "I thought you said she was all right."

Patterson grimaced, not completely convinced that the intruder's target wasn't this woman.

Andy headed for the door. "I'll go check on her," he told Millie.

"I'll go with you," Patterson chimed in.

"Good!" Ariana shoved a hand on her hip. "Millie can stay and help me clean up this mess!"

Patterson and Andy passed Pierre on his way in. His eyes scanned the mess. "What happened Ariana? Did you have another meltdown?" he smirked.

Ariana flipped him the bird. "No! For your information, someone broke into my room and whacked Kay on the head."

She stood upright and flounced over to the small makeup counter near the balcony door. "Here, help me get these pins out of my hair."

"That is Kay's job," he pointed out.

"Kay is not here," Ariana argued.

Pierre knew he wouldn't win the battle with his boss and promptly began to pull the bobby pins from her hair.

Millie reached down and picked up a pair of shoes. She opened the closet door and dropped them on the floor.

She turned in time to see Pierre yank a pin from Ariana's hair. "Ouch! Watch what you're doing! That hurt!"

The battle between the two continued for several long moments until Ariana's long tresses tumbled around her shoulders and Pierre started for the door. "I'll go check on Kay now."

Ariana didn't bother to respond, or even thank Pierre, as she stomped off to the small bathroom. She stepped inside and slammed the door behind her.

Millie picked up a stack of books and laid them on the small bookshelf. "Did you see anything, Pierre?"

Pierre reached for the door handle. "No, Millie. I was backstage with Ariana the whole time."

She nodded and Pierre stepped outside, quietly closing the door behind him.

Ariana stayed inside the bathroom for what seemed like forever...long enough for Millie to straighten the entire suite. Finally, Ariana emerged. Millie wondered if she hid out in the bath so she wouldn't have to clean the mess.

The woman had removed most of the caked on stage makeup. She had changed into a pair of skinny jeans and silky coral blouse. On her feet were hot pink stilettos.

Millie narrowed her eyes and set the TV remote on the makeup counter. "Are you going somewhere?"

Ariana tilted her head. "No, not really. I thought maybe you and I could run down to karaoke and perhaps check out the competition." She smiled.

"Sure." Millie had no plans. No. Millie had no *life* – not until Ariana was gone, anyway. "Let me run to the bathroom."

She reached for the bathroom door handle and gave Ariana a warning look. "I'll be right out."

Inside the small space, Millie hurried as fast as she could. She quickly washed her hands and stepped out of the bathroom.

Her heart lurched when her eyes fell on the end of the sofa...the spot where Ariana had just been sitting. The woman was long gone and the room empty.

Chapter 6

Millie picked up her radio and pressed the button. "Andy, do you copy?"

"Go ahead, Millie."

She swallowed hard and squeezed her eyes shut. "Ariana took off again."

There was a long pause on the other end. Millie could almost hear the string of cuss words. She didn't dare tell Andy that all she did was use the restroom and the woman vanished...again!

"I'll start looking right now," she promised.

She took one last glance around the suite before she stepped outside and closed the door behind her. Maybe she had tired of waiting the few milliseconds it took Millie to use the restroom and had headed to the karaoke bar.

It was wishful thinking on Millie's part. She walked through the entire karaoke bar. Ariana was not inside. She stopped by the piano bar on her way down the long corridor. The room was full of guests but none of them was Ariana.

She looked inside the casino. No Ariana. The liquor store. Nada. She started past Ocean Treasures gift shop and made a last minute decision to check with Cat.

The place was deader than a doornail. Cat watched as Millie made her way to the back. She stuck her elbow on the counter and studied her friend's expression. "Why the glum face?"

"Ariana. She's MIA again!"

Cat tipped her head to the side thoughtfully. "What does she look like again?"

"Willowy blonde…kinda tall. She was wearing a pink shirt and blue jeans."

Cat raised a brow. "I think I saw her a few minutes ago. Was she with a good-looking man, about her height with jet black hair, a little on the long side and pulled back in a ponytail?"

"No." Millie frowned. "That couldn't be her."

Cat shrugged. "The only reason I noticed is they seemed to be arguing. The woman stalked off with the man chasing after her."

That part sounded like Ariana, to a "T"!

Cat snapped her fingers. "Hey. We have a small surveillance camera near the door. Maybe it caught them on camera."

Millie followed Cat to the back storage room. She kept an eye out for shoppers as Cat fiddled with the video machine.

Cat shifted the recorder and stared at the screen. "Yeah. They're on here. Take a look."

Millie pulled her reading glasses from her front pocket and slipped them on. Sure enough, Ariana was standing in front of the gift shop, arguing with a man that Millie didn't recognize.

"That's her." Millie jabbed her finger on the screen. "But I've never seen that man before."

She reached for her radio. "Andy, do you copy?"

"Tell me you found her." Andy's voice crackled over the airwaves.

"Nope, but I have something important to show you. Meet me in Ocean Treasures."

Moments later, Andy strolled into the shop. "This better be good," he warned.

Millie led him to the back storage room. She pressed the button on the machine and played the video. Andy rewound the tape and watched it a second time. "Who is that man with Ariana?"

"Good question," Millie answered.

"I'll have security search for her," Andy said.

Millie shook her head. "I don't think that's necessary. In fact, I'm guessing that Ariana is hiding out in Tahitian Nights."

Tahitian Nights was the dance club for the 20 something to 30 something crowd. It was one of the few spots on the ship where someone...a couple, perhaps, could hide out.

Millie stormed out of the gift shop and strode across the hall. She climbed the three flights of stair with Andy hot on her heels. He wished he could give Ariana Teliar a swift kick in the rear for all the trouble she was causing.

He glanced at Millie out of the corner of his eye. That might not be necessary, judging by the look on Millie's face.

Brody, the bouncer, stood near the entrance to the club. He studied Millie's brooding expression and then grinned. "Millie, you look madder than a wet hornet."

Millie blew air through her thinned lips. "I am. Have you seen a pretty blonde, about this tall, come in here with a man wearing a cheap leisure suit and long dark hair pulled back in a ponytail?"

Brody tucked his hands behind his back. "Yep. I had to card her and she had a hissy fit. Pretty thing. Not sure what she was doing with that guy."

He jerked his head. "They're off in the corner."

She pointed to Brody's flashlight. "Mind if I borrow that?"

"Be my guest." Brody unsnapped the fastener that held the flashlight in place and stuck it in Millie's outstretched hand.

"Thanks." Millie swung the door open and stepped inside the dark bar. Loud, techno music thumped in the air. A throng of gyrating bodies filled the dance floor.

Andy and Millie stayed close to the edge of the dance floor as they made their way to the back corner.

When they got to the corner, Millie tipped the flashlight and pointed it toward the floor. She flipped the button on the side and then quickly shone the light on the occupants in the corner.

The light beamed into Ariana's eyes and temporarily blinded her. She clamped her hand over her eyes. "Turn that thing off!" she shouted.

Millie ignored her and turned the flashlight on the man sitting next to her. He held an arm over his eyes and cursed.

Millie reached for Ariana's arm. "Let's go outside."

The man attempted to come to Ariana's aid and leaned forward. "Let her go."

Andy stopped him. "You best stay out of this," he warned.

Millie retraced her steps with Ariana by her side. Andy and the unidentified man followed them out.

They passed Brody, who stood sentinel outside the entrance. Millie handed him his flashlight. "Thanks."

She pulled Ariana off to the side before she released her grip. "What are you doing and who is he?" She pointed to the man.

"We are fr-," he started to say.

Ariana cut him off. "We just met," she raised her chin in defiance.

"I don't believe you," Millie hissed through clenched teeth. "Try again."

Ariana clamped her mouth shut and crossed her arms.

The man reached out to touch her arm. "Ariana..."

She gave him a dark look. "Shut up!"

Andy placed a hand on the man's shoulder. "You might as well come clean now. If not, you can come clean later while you're sitting in a jail cell, charged with kidnapping."

"Christopher did not kidnap me," Ariana insisted.

"Christopher. We're getting somewhere," Andy observed.

Christopher's shoulders sagged. "Christopher Johnson. I'm Ariana's boyfriend."

Millie gasped. "You brought your boyfriend onboard?"

Sudden tears filled Ariana's eyes. She clasped her hands together. "Please don't tell anyone. Daddy will be furious if he finds out."

The pieces were all starting to fall into place. Ariana's boyfriend had snuck on the ship, which was why Ariana kept disappearing...so she could spend time with her boyfriend whom "daddy" aka Mr. Moneybags, didn't approve.

"Your father doesn't like Mr. Johnson?" Andy asked.

"No! He hates him!" Ariana began to cry. She buried her hands in her face.

"It's okay, Ariana." Christopher put an arm around her shoulder. "I'm sure they won't tell your father."

Ariana wailed for several long moments. Millie darted into the bathroom and returned carrying a roll of toilet paper, the only thing she could find.

Ariana dabbed at the streaks of mascara that ran down her cheeks. "Please don't tell anyone. I'm begging you."

"Pierre and Kay don't know?" Millie asked.

Ariana shook her head. "No. They work for daddy and will report back."

Millie, not one to stand in the way of true love, if that's what it was, agreed to keep quiet. Andy did, too, but he was reluctant. If Mr. Teliar/Gatwick found out they withheld information, he could try to have them both fired.

Millie and Andy left the two lovebirds alone for a moment to say good-bye. Andy jerked his head in their direction. "Now what?"

"I'll take care of it," Millie told him. "You stay out of this. At least if they're found out, you can claim ignorance." She had a point.

On the way back to the suite, Millie had a serious conversation with Ariana, who agreed not to disappear without telling Millie where she was going, as long as Millie let Ariana spend time with Christopher.

In theory, it was a great idea. If only Ariana would keep end of the bargain.

Chapter 7

The rest of the evening was quiet and uneventful, if not somewhat uncomfortable…at least for Millie, who couldn't find a comfortable position on the cot to save her life.

Every time she moved, the springs creaked loudly. If they weren't creaking, they were stabbing her in the back, her legs and even her shoulder blades.

Millie vowed she would never again complain about her small bunk bed.

Ariana, who had a spacious queen size bed, snored softly and slept like a bear in hibernation.

Millie awoke early the next morning groggy – and cranky. The room was quiet and Millie slowly opened one eye. Ariana's bed was empty.

She bolted upright in the cot as her eyes scanned the room. She threw back the covers and her feet touched the floor.

Millie could feel the tips of her ears burn and her face redden. She jammed her feet into her slippers and slowly stood when she heard a noise. Someone was humming and the sound was coming from the bathroom.

The bathroom door popped open and a fresh-faced, wide-eyed, smiling Ariana emerged. "Good morning, sleepyhead," she said cheerfully.

Millie smiled, despite her aching back and stiff neck. "Good morning, Ariana. You look chipper today."

Millie reached for her backpack and shuffled to the bathroom. Coffee. She needed coffee.

Although Millie hated the cot, she loved Ariana's shower, which was large and luxurious. Millie was even able to bend over without having the shower curtain cling to parts of her body. She stepped out of the bathroom in much better spirits than when she went in.

The door that separated Ariana's and Kay's cabin was open. "Is Kay here?"

Ariana shook her head. "Nope. She was already gone when I got up."

She quickly changed the subject. "Can we go to the dining room for breakfast? Christopher is waiting."

Millie nodded. "Sure." She slipped her lanyard around her neck and the girls headed out the door.

The dining room was busy but Ariana was still able to spot Christopher sitting near the front of the restaurant. He waved them over and Ariana slid into the seat across from him.

Millie, not wanting to intrude on the lovebirds, sat alone at the booth behind them. She could count on one hand the number of times she'd eaten in the dining room, which was a total of two, counting today.

The items on the menu all sounded good and Millie made the difficult decision to try the cinnamon waffles. She ordered a side of bacon and a side of potato wedges to go along with the waffles. The food was delicious and the coffee was the most flavorful she'd had since she began working onboard Siren of the Seas.

Millie sliced off a chunk of syrupy goodness and popped the treat into her mouth. Today was a port day. The ship would dock on the shores of Costa Maya. Millie had never been to Costa Maya and she wondered what Ariana...and Christopher, whom she had a feeling would be tagging along, wanted to do.

She shifted in her seat so that she faced their booth. "What are we doing today?"

Ariana lifted her coffee cup and took a sip. "I want to visit Mayan ruins but decided to wait until we reached Cozumel." She paused. "How does ziplining sound?"

Millie's heart plummeted. Ziplining? Visions of the line breaking and Millie hurtling to earth at 100 miles per hour flashed before her eyes. She shook her head. Even if the line didn't break, the rush of adrenaline would most likely give her a heart attack.

Ariana saw the look of terror in Millie's eyes and quickly dismissed ziplining. "Cave tubing?" she asked hopefully.

Millie wasn't thrilled with that suggestion, either, but if she had to decide between the lesser of the two evils, it was definitely keeping both feet on the ground...or in this case, floating in the water. "I suppose."

She wondered if perhaps Cat or Annette wanted to go with them. Millie quickly finished her food and wiped her mouth with the cloth napkin next to her plate. "I need to make a quick stop. Meet me next to the gangplank in half an hour."

Christopher smiled, the dimple on his chin deepening. "Sure, Millie...and thanks again."

Millie stopped by the gift shop first. Her heart sank when she saw Cat working. She crossed Cat off her list and headed to the kitchen.

Annette was inside, surrounded by jars of spices. "Where are you headed?" Annette eyed Millie's casual attire.

"Cave tubing," she announced glumly. "I was hoping you could go with me."

Annette set the container of garlic powder on the counter. "Sounds like fun but I can't today. How 'bout we do something tomorrow?"

Tomorrow the ship would dock in Cozumel. Ariana had mentioned Mayan Ruins. "Mayan Ruins?" she asked hopefully.

Annette pounded the piece of chicken on the counter with the tenderizer. "Sure. Sounds like fun."

Millie jogged back to her own cabin in search of a bathing suit and water shoes. She changed into a swimsuit and then slipped into an old t-shirt and pair of shorts. She dropped her lanyard around her neck and headed out the door. She prayed all the way to the gangway, that she wouldn't get lost in the cave or worse yet, get bit by an Anaconda.

Millie was relieved when she spied Ariana near the gangplank. Christopher was several yards away. Millie almost didn't recognize him in his dark sunglasses and long hair, which now hung loosely around his shoulders.

Ariana handed a ticket to Millie. "I paid for the excursion already," she explained.

Millie took the ticket. "Thank you. I think."

Ariana patted her arm. "Don't worry. It'll be fun."

The tour guide lifted his paddle high above his head and the group followed him down the long dock to a waiting bus. At least the bus was newer and had air-conditioning, Millie thought to herself.

After the seats filled and the bus pulled away from the curb, the guide, who stood at the front of the bus and faced the passengers, began to speak.

"Ladies and gentlemen, today we will travel far into the rainforest, to the edge of the Chua River. Chua means snake and there are a few snakes in the river where we'll be tubing."

Millie turned her terror-filled eyes to Ariana. "Snakes? What kind of snakes?" She decided right then and there that her fears were not so foolish, after all.

"Although most of our snakes are harmless, we do have vipers that will strike if provoked. They prefer to sunbathe on the banks of the river because the water is cold. Same thing with the alligators."

"Alligators?" Millie started to stand. This bus needed to turn around because this girl was not about to swim with snakes and alligators!

Ariana tugged on her arm. "You'll be fine. Just stay away from the banks of the river."

Millie hadn't been on an inner tube since she was a teenager. What if the water was more like racing rapids than meandering stream? Images of bumping into the banks and a snake slithering onto her inner tube filled her mind.

"...we will hike to the top of the hill, across a few small streams until we get to the river."

Before Millie could digest this latest tidbit of information, the bus came to an abrupt halt.

The tour guide pulled the silver handle that opened the door. "We will complete the next leg of our journey in the other bus."

Millie peered out the front window and at the backside of what looked like an old school bus. The passengers shuffled down the narrow aisle, stepped off the shiny, new bus and climbed aboard the older, rundown bus.

The first thing Millie noticed was the hot, humid air. Despite the fact that all of the windows were wide open, the air was stagnant and sticky.

She followed Ariana onto the bus and the two women settled into the seat behind Christopher, who seemed delighted with the turn of events. "This ought to be fun. I haven't ridden in a school bus since I was a kid."

Millie shifted on the cheap vinyl seat. Between this trip and the cot she slept on the previous night, Millie could envision a visit to the chiropractor in the near future.

After everyone settled in, the guide closed the door and the bus lurched forward. The dirt road was riddled with deep ruts and they bounced up and down for several agonizing miles.

The oppressive humidity and motion caused Millie to feel queasy. She closed her eyes and leaned her head back.

"Are you okay?" Ariana whispered in her ear.

"No. I think I'm going to throw up."

"Don't do it on me," Ariana shuddered unsympathetically.

Thankfully, the bus finally stopped and the guide spoke. "We are here to begin our next part of the journey."

The passengers exited the bus and clustered in small groups off to the side. Millie glanced at the other passengers. Her whole purpose of this trip was to keep Ariana safe. She studied the group with interest.

Was someone on this excursion here for the sole purpose of taking Ariana out? Would they have the guts to try something in the middle of the rainforest?

Maybe it was the heat, but everyone began to look suspicious. Her eyes wandered to Christopher. Maybe it was Christopher. The three of them waited in a long line while the guide handed out inner tubes.

"We have to carry the tube?" This excursion was getting better by the minute.

The guide overhead Millie. "Yes, ma'am. You must carry your tube with you."

Millie grabbed her tube and followed behind Ariana as she began her ascent up the side of the mountain. The winding path was narrow and riddled with long vines that hung down. The vines reminded Millie of snakes and she shivered despite the stifling humidity.

She kept one eye on the vines and the other on the path where tree roots poked up out of the ground causing her to stumble. The walk, mixed with the hot, muggy air was almost unbearable and Millie was suffering.

She had convinced herself that this excursion could not possibly get any worse…until the group reached the creek.

The guide, who was in the lead, stopped. "We must cross here. Hold onto your tube. Do not let go or else you will be forced to swim after it!"

Millie made her way to the edge of the water and watched the first few brave souls cross. They made it look easy. The guide stood in the center of the stream and encouraged each person who trekked across the open waters.

Christopher was the first in their small group to cross. He waded through the water as if it wasn't even there. When he reached the other side, he gave the girls the thumbs up.

Ariana was next. The cold water splashed her upper thighs and the inner tube started to slip from her grasp.

The guide cupped his hands around his mouth. "Don't let go of the tube!"

Ariana nodded as she attempted to secure the tube under her arm.

Millie held her breath until she reached the other side, safe and sound.

Millie let a couple of the others in the group go ahead of her as she tried to determine the safest and easiest spot to cross. She decided that if she started a little to the left, it might be a quicker trek.

Finally, it was Millie's turn. She sucked in a breath. "Here goes nothing," she muttered. The water was ice cold and goose bumps sprouted on her legs and arms. As much as she would have liked to, she knew there was no turning back so she pressed on.

She slowly shuffled forward, keeping both eyes on the goal...the bank on the other side. A couple times, she felt as if something, probably a snake, was trying to wrap itself around her legs but when she glanced down into the crystal-clear water, all she could see were tree roots.

When Millie reached the halfway point, the guide cheered her on. "You are doing a good job grandma."

Millie frowned. Did he think that Millie was Ariana's grandmother? Well...technically, she probably could be...

Millie, distracted by the comment and feeling a little more confident, let her guard down, which was a mistake.

She stepped on a mossy rock and the rubber sole of her water shoe slipped on the slimy surface. She fought to regain her balance, her arms flailed wildly in the air. She released her grip on the tube and watched in horror as the tube bounced off the water and began to dance down the creek!

The guide lunged for the tube. Millie tried to get out of the way and jerked to the side where she finally lost her balance and plunged into the icy water, face first.

Millie panicked as she thrashed around in the water, trying desperately to get back on her feet. Strong arms lifted her from the water and half-carried, half-dragged her to the other side.

The crowd began to cheer. Millie wiped the water from her face and gazed at her rescuer. It was Christopher!

The guide brought up the rear, carrying Millie's tube.

Millie thanked the guide and then blinked back tears as she thanked Christopher.

"You made it." The guide waved them forward. "We are almost there."

Millie, who had had her fill of adventure, could hardly wait!

Chapter 8

The view from the top of the hill was breathtaking. Millie's eyes were drawn to a majestic waterfall across the ravine, the water cascading over the sides and pouring into an emerald lagoon far below. The sun hit the mist of water at just the right angle and a rainbow appeared.

Millie took a deep breath and closed her eyes. A rainbow...God's promise she would survive this adventure.

With a renewed sense of determination and the knowledge that this would be her first and last attempt at cave tubing, she joined the group as they crowded the riverbank.

Christopher and Ariana were already in the water, their tubes nearing the cave entrance. Millie, determined not to let them out of her sight, quickly dropped her tube in the water and plopped on top. She shoved off from the edge as she remembered the guide's warning that snakes liked to sunbathe along the banks.

Christopher and Ariana disappeared inside the cave and Millie lost her visual. She stuck both hands in the water and began to paddle as she frantically tried to catch up.

Someone suddenly bumped the back of her tube. Millie turned to see a gray haired man wearing a red tank top and two sizes too small swim trunks directly behind her. "Pretty cool adventure."

Millie, now certain that she would survive the excursion, had to admit it was somewhat fun. How many people could say they went cave tubing in the middle of a rainforest?

He pointed to the top of the cave. "Those look like bats."

Millie followed his gaze to the cave ceiling. He was right. Above them were several clumps of dark, furry objects.

The guide floated by. "Yes, those are our resident bats."

Millie shivered and began to paddle to the side of the cave so she wasn't directly underneath them. The cave was cool and refreshing. If not for the bats, Millie probably would have hung off to the side and enjoyed a brief break.

The man followed her lead. "Are you on this excursion alone?"

Millie swallowed the lump that had lodged in her throat. Great! The guy was hitting on her!

She shook her head. "No. My friends are up ahead. In fact, I need to catch up with them."

She didn't wait for his reply as she paddled off in search of Christopher and Ariana.

Millie caught a glimpse of them up ahead, just before they rounded a bend and disappeared from sight. By the time Millie rounded the bend, they were gone!

She craned her neck as she tried to see around the other tubers. It was as if they had vanished. She spent the rest of the journey trying to track them down and by the time the guide waved them off the river, Millie was exhausted.

She slid out of the tube and grabbed the edge as she tugged the tube behind her and waded to shore.

Millie edged her way through the crowd. It suddenly occurred to her that the two of them had vanished – on purpose!

Millie clenched her jaw and trudged along with the group as they made their way back down the side of the mountain to the waiting school bus. Much to her surprise – or maybe it wasn't – Ariana and Christopher were the last two to join the group as they brought up the rear.

She marched over to them and shoved Christopher, who had his back to Millie. "What's the big idea taking off like that? I just spent the last two hours trying to find you two!" she fumed.

Ariana could see Millie was hot under the collar and tried to smooth things over. "I'm sorry Millie. I had to go to the bathroom so we stopped off. By the time we got back in the water, you had already passed by so we ended up behind you."

Millie frowned. She didn't buy that excuse for a single second. No one in their right mind would wander off in the jungle for a bathroom break, knowing it was full of snakes, gators and heaven knew what else!

She grunted, turned on her heel and stomped onto the bus. Millie settled in by the window and closed her eyes.

Ariana tried to talk to Millie on the way back to the ship but finally gave up when she realized the best thing she could do was to give her a chance to calm down.

Millie eventually did cool off. By the time the bus parked outside the dock, Millie had forgiven Christopher and Ariana. She hadn't forgotten, but she had forgiven them.

The group shuffled off the bus single file with Millie right behind Christopher. Christopher stopped to hand the guide a few dollars tip as Millie and Ariana waited off to the side. The girls watched as several of the other passengers did the same.

Christopher shoved his wallet in his back pocket. "Ready?"

Ariana's eyes widened and she clutched at Christopher's arm. "Oh my gosh! There's Firkin!"

Millie followed her gaze. Ariana was staring at the gray haired man who had tried to strike up a conversation with Millie inside the cave. She had

thought he was hitting on her but maybe not...
"Who is Firkin?"

"I-I can't tell you right now. Please don't ask me," Ariana begged. Millie could see the Firkin-fellow had Ariana rattled.

Christopher groaned. "How did he get here?"

Firkin must have felt their eyes on him. He turned to look directly at them. He lifted his hand, pointed his index finger and then bent his thumb, as if pulling the trigger of a gun.

Christopher and Ariana kept a close eye on Firkin as they headed to the gangway to board the ship. The young couple appeared to be in a big hurry to make it through security and put some distance between them and the mysterious man, "Firkin."

Christopher came to an abrupt halt near the elevators. "I'll stay here to see if he boards."

Ariana nodded. "Good idea."

Christopher pointed to Ariana's fanny pack, hooked around her waist. "You got everything?"

She patted the front. "Yep."

Millie's eyes narrowed. Something funny was going on here and she was determined to get to the bottom of it.

Ariana and she started for the stairs. Millie made a grab for the bag. "What's in the bag, Ariana?"

Ariana jerked back and stuck a protective hand over the top. "Nothing."

"Does it have something to do with Christopher and you disappearing in the jungle?"

Ariana snorted. "Yeah, right. Maybe I brought a souvenir snake back with me. Here wanna check?" She began to unclip the bag from her waist.

As much as Millie was dying to find out what might be in the bag, she wasn't quite that brave.

When they reached the suite, Ariana plucked her key card from the small zippered compartment in the front and inserted the key in the door.

She pushed it open and Millie followed her inside.

Kay was in the suite, sitting in a corner chair, a steely expression on her face. "Where did you two sneak off to all day?"

Ariana shrugged nonchalantly. "Oh, just a little cave tubing adventure." She peeled off her wet t-shirt and slipped out of her water shoes. "We didn't bother asking since I knew you weren't fond of water...or snakes."

Kay's eyes glittered and she popped out of the chair. "I love swimming and if Millie can handle snakes, so can I," she shot back.

Millie took a step back. She had never seen Kay look so angry. "I'm sorry we didn't ask you,

Kay. After the bump on the head yesterday, I thought you would want to rest."

"Well, you thought wrong," Kay hissed. Realizing she sounded like a shrew, she backed off. "I sat here all by myself, bored out of my mind."

"We'll be sure to invite you next time," Millie promised. Maybe the bump on her head made her cranky.

Ariana smiled, grabbed some clean clothes from the drawer and headed into the bathroom. Unfortunately, for Millie, she took her fanny pack with her!

Millie needed to run down to her own cabin for a clean uniform. She turned to Kay. "Will you be here for a few minutes?"

"I won't let her out of my sight," Kay promised.

Millie headed out of the suite and made her way back to her cabin. Something was not adding up. Ariana and Christopher disappeared in the jungle for a reason. Someone had ransacked Ariana's room...searching for something. If they had just wanted to kill her, why tear her room apart?

Now there was this mysterious "Firkin." Who was Firkin and why was he following them?

It seemed as if the more time she spent around Ariana, the less she knew her.

She was relieved to find her own cabin empty. It would give her a few moments of peace and quiet to mull over what she knew.

Tomorrow was another port day – Cozumel. She remembered Ariana telling her she wanted to visit the Mayan ruins. Millie decided she would be accompanying Ariana and vowed not let her out of her sight!

The ship would be in Costa Maya for another couple of hours, which meant the ship's internet connection would be much faster than when the ship was at sea.

She quickly finished showering and dressing and then headed to the business center.

The computer stations were empty. Millie slid into one of the stations in the back. She logged onto her email account, read a few messages from her children and then began a search.

She remembered Andy telling her that Ariana's father, Gatwick, was some sort of real estate mogul. She clicked on the search bar and typed in "Gatwick" and "real estate." Several search results appeared and Millie clicked on the first one that came up.

"Jacob Gatwick, financier who specializes in archeology expeditions, recently alluded to plans to start a major dig in Central America, namely in the region of Quintana Roo. Experts speculate that Mr. Gatwick stumbled upon a piece of the missing Mayan dynasty, which could lead to the discovery of Palenque, thought to be the ancient civilization's industrial and gold capitol."

The article continued:

"If this proves true, Mr. Gatwick's project could unearth rare treasures that would undoubtedly make him the richest man in the world."

Millie squinted at the date of the article. It was less than two months old! She leaned back in the chair, her head spinning. Had Gatwick sent his daughter in search of the treasure? Why wouldn't he just send his own people...unless, of course, his daughter was an archaeologist.

Millie placed her fingers on the keyboard and typed in "Ariana Gatwick." An image of a young woman, standing next to an older gentleman appeared on the screen.

Millie slipped her glasses on. The caption underneath read: Jacob Gatwick and daughter, Ariana Gatwick."

Millie double clicked to enlarge the photo. The young woman was tall and blonde and at first glance, it looked like Ariana.

There was something different about the woman. She studied the photo closely. It was on the edge of her mind. She shifted her gaze to the passengers who were chattering at each other across the hall.

Millie turned back to study the photo. The young woman, whose arms were in front of her, clutched a small glittery handbag.

Millie pulled her phone from her back pocket and held it up to the screen. She snapped a couple quick photos and then shoved the camera back in her pocket.

The woman in the photo had an odd-shaped birthmark or scar above her wrist.

Millie was convinced that the woman she knew as Ariana did not have that mark!

Chapter 9

Millie's first impulse was to march up to Ariana's suite and demand an explanation, but Millie had a sneaky suspicion that might backfire on her. She needed to build a case, figure out who this imposter was and why she was posing as Ariana Teliar.

Millie decided she needed some help and who better to ask than Cat and Annette. Millie knew the gift shop would not open for at least another hour, until the ship sailed out of port. The kitchen would be slow because most of the guests were still on shore or just coming back.

She stopped by Cat's cabin first and knocked on the door.

A bleary-eyed Cat answered. Millie grinned at the sight of her bouffant hairdo looking a little off kilter and rough around the edges. "Hey Millie."

"I'm sorry to wake you," Millie apologized. "I need some advice."

Cat held the door open. "C'mon in."

Millie followed her inside the dark cabin. "I was hoping I could talk to Annette and you at the same time."

Cat flipped on a small light over the desk. She held up a finger. "Sure. Just give me a minute to freshen up." She disappeared inside the small bathroom and Millie looked around. She'd only been in Cat's cabin once before. She knew Cat had a cabin mate but she'd never met the person.

When Cat emerged from the bathroom, Millie started to ask her if she'd heard anything else on Jay but changed her mind. Jay was Cat's ex-husband. He had sent her an empty envelope a couple weeks ago and the girls were concerned that since he had been able to track her down, he would also try to sneak onboard the ship to finish what he'd started...to murder Cat, his ex-wife.

Cat had notified Dave Patterson and ship security. The ship's passenger list now had to pass through a special screening process as they searched for Jay Beck's name. So far, there had been no sign of him and he had made no other attempt to contact her.

Cat was not lulled into a sense of false security. She knew it wasn't a matter of "if" Jay showed up but a matter of "when."

Millie decided not to mention Jay's name and the girls wandered up the steps and into the kitchen.

Annette was in the far corner having what appeared to be a serious conversation with her right hand man, Amit. When Annette saw the girls, she told Amit she'd talk to him later.

"Trouble in Annette's kitchen?" Cat smirked.

"Nothing that a little pep talk can't take care of," Annette said. "So what brings you two to my neck of the woods?"

Annette suddenly remembered that Millie had invited her to go cave tubing. "How was cave tubing?"

Millie frowned. "That's why I'm here. Do you have a minute?"

"Sure. Let's go to the conference room."

Annette led the way to the walk-in pantry. It looked as if they had just restocked and there were several rows of freshly baked cookies.

Millie eyed the cookies as her stomach grumbled. She hadn't eaten since breakfast and the day's activities had left her famished.

Annette motioned to the cookies. "Help yourself."

"Thanks." Millie reached for a container of chocolate chip cookies. She pulled one from the package and then offered one to Cat, who shook her head.

Millie bit the end of the cookie. The creamy milk chocolate chip and crisp cookie edge melted in her mouth. "Oh my gosh! These are so good!"

"Thanks. So what's up?" Annette prompted.

Millie started at the beginning and explained how Andy had told her she was to stick with Ariana for the entire time she was onboard the ship. She explained how they had found Miguel's body on Ariana's balcony and how someone had attacked Kay and then ransacked Ariana's room.

Millie shook her head. "Now there are strange people popping up from out of nowhere, including her 'boyfriend' Christopher and some guy named Firkin."

She popped the rest of the cookie in her mouth. "On top of that, I'm not sure this woman's real name is Ariana Teliar / Gatwick."

"Why not?" Cat asked.

"Because I just searched her father's name on the internet. The man is wealthy as all get out.

His hobby is financing archaeology digs and they recently reported that he was onto something. Some lost Mayan civilization. Guess where it's at?"

"In Mexico?"

"Bingo!" Millie said. "Funny thing that Ariana and her boyfriend disappeared during the excursion, then suddenly reappeared, along with this other guy, Firkin."

Annette offered Millie another cookie and when Millie shook her head, she sealed the package shut and shoved it back on the shelf. "What's your take? They're all after the same thing?"

"That's what I'm thinking," Millie said. "On top of that, I don't think the woman that I'm watching is even Ariana, the daughter."

Cat shifted her feet. "Then who is she?"

"Good question," Millie said. "The real Ariana has a scar on top of her wrist. After I leave here,

I'm headed up there to find out if the woman I know to be Ariana has the same scar."

"What's the plan? Try to flush her out?" Annette loved a good mystery and this one showed promise.

"I have a sneaky suspicion that Ariana is going to try to ditch me tomorrow and head over to the Mayan ruins near Tulum."

Annette's eye gleamed. "I have tomorrow off. I'd love to help."

Cat nodded. "Me, too. Sounds like you're onto something."

"That's what I was hoping," Millie sounded relieved. "My only problem is that if she gives me the slip, how will I find her?"

Annette snapped her fingers. "I have something that will fix her little red wagon. Stay here." She darted out of the storage room and disappeared around the corner.

Veronica Chang, one of the kitchen crew and not one of Millie's favorite, flounced into the closet. "What are you doing here?"

"Guarding the cookies," Millie joked.

Veronica rolled her eyes, grabbed a large bag of powdered sugar and stalked out of the room.

Millie watched her go. "She is such a party pooper."

Annette returned a short time later. "Here. Take this." She held her hand out to Millie.

Millie watched as Annette dropped a small metal disc in the palm of her hand. It was the size of Millie's fingernail.

Millie brought it close to her face. "What is it?"

"A tracking device. You'll have to find a spot to hide it where Ariana will be sure to take it with her tomorrow. That way, if she takes off, we'll be able to track her down."

Millie turned the small device over in her hand. "Where do you get this stuff?"

Annette smiled mysteriously. "Sorry Millie. If I told you that, I'd have to kill you," she joked.

Millie gave Annette a quick hug. "Thanks for loaning the tracker. I hope I get it back in one piece."

Annette shrugged. "Don't worry. There are more where that came from."

Cat and Millie wandered out of the storage room and then out of the kitchen. They stopped in the hall. "Be careful, Millie," Cat fretted. "You don't know who you're dealing with. These people sound ruthless."

"I will," Millie reassured her friend. For all they knew, Ariana could be the mastermind behind some sort of illegal operation.

Millie shoved the small tracker in her front pants pocket and headed to the theater. She turned toward Ariana's suite and then changed her mind. Instead, she decided to stop by Andy's office to check in.

She knew that soon he would have to make his way down to the gangway and greet the final stragglers coming back from Costa Maya.

A small lump lodged in her throat when she saw the top of Andy's head, bent over his work area. She missed her routine, her friends and Scout. This business of babysitting was getting her down.

"Hey there." She didn't want to sneak up on him and scare him half to death.

Andy lifted his head. He grinned. "Hello Millie. Miss me?"

"Yes. As a matter of fact I do."

Andy pulled his reading glasses off and set them on top of his notepad. "I miss you, too. I also appreciate you sticking with Ariana. I know she's a real handful."

Millie groaned as she sank into the chair next to Andy. "Brother, that woman is a handful on steroids. Just keeping a visual on her is a full time job. She keeps sneaking off."

"With the boyfriend?" Andy prompted.

Millie glanced around to see if anyone was in earshot. "I don't think this woman is on the up-and-up."

"Do you think that she's responsible for Miguel's death?" Andy raised a brow.

Millie rubbed an imaginary spot on the desk. "I don't think so but I'm not ruling it out. I'm onto something and hopefully getting close to figuring out what's going on."

"Just be careful," Andy warned. "You have a penchant for getting yourself into sticky situations."

"I will." Millie smoothed her index finger over the small disc in her pocket. With any luck, the girls would be cracking this case wide open in less than 24 hours!

Chapter 10

Kay answered the door when Millie knocked. She motioned Millie inside. "Is she here?"

"Yep." Kay nodded. "I haven't let her out of my sight. She's outside."

Millie wandered out onto the balcony. She found Ariana lounging in one of the deck chairs. The petite blonde was wearing a pair of dark sunglasses and reading her Kindle. "Whatcha reading?"

Ariana snapped the cover shut and shoved her sunglasses on top of her head. "*Fairly Common*. It's about a girl who is kidnapped and held for ransom."

Millie lifted a brow. "Sounds interesting."

Ariana agreed. "And exciting."

Millie plopped down in the chair next to Ariana, her eyes drawn to the woman's wrist.

There, above her right wrist was a mark. It looked lighter than the one in the picture, but it was there. Millie impulsively reached out and rubbed the top of the mark. "Why I never noticed that mark before, Ariana."

Ariana quickly snatched her arm from Millie's grasp and covered the spot. "Just a little birthmark," she said.

Millie had made her nervous. She quickly shot out of the chair and headed for the door. "I don't know about you but I'm starving."

Kay, who was in her own cabin with the door ajar, emerged when she heard the balcony door open.

"We're getting ready to go grab a bite to eat," Millie said. "You want to come?"

Kay grabbed her keycard and shoved it into her pocket. "Of course. I'm not letting Ariana out of my sight."

Ariana shrugged her shoulders. "Okay, let's go."

The women strolled across the dark theater as they made their way out into the hall and down to the Blue Seas dining room.

The hostess seated them by the window and Millie was mesmerized by the magnificent ocean view. Her mind began to wander and she wondered how often Captain Armati ate in the dining room. She had heard mention of passengers who were invited to dine at the Captain's Table and then she wondered if any of the single women onboard ever flirted with him.

She quickly dismissed the thought. Millie liked the captain...more than she cared to admit. Still, it was none of her business whose company he kept.

Ariana interrupted her thoughts. "The menu looks interesting."

Millie picked hers up, slipped her reading glasses on and studied the choices. She had a hard time deciding. Everything looked good. It didn't help that she was starving. The cookie she'd eaten earlier was long gone.

Millie recognized the waiter but couldn't remember his name. She glanced at his tag. Kenneth.

Ariana chose the iceberg wedge with blue cheese as an appetizer and then the filet mignon for her main dish.

Kay, whose tastes were simpler, opted for a tossed salad and lasagna Bolognese.

Millie was the last to order. She finally decided on the French onion soup and roasted chicken with a side of red potatoes.

The waiter set a basket of bread in the center of the table and a tin of butter right next to it. Millie's mouth watered as she reached for the basket. The bread was soft and warm, as if it had just come from the oven.

She ate three pieces before her soup arrived. By the time Kenneth set the plate of chicken in front of her, she was starting to feel full. Not wanting to waste good food, she managed to eat every single morsel.

When Kenneth returned with dessert menus, much to Millie's dismay, she had to pass. She couldn't fit one more bite in her mouth.

Ariana and Kay both ordered the tiramisu, and while they waited for the desserts to arrive, Millie decided it was time to corner Ariana about her plans for the following day.

She sipped her coffee and studied Ariana over the rim. "We're going to the Mayan ruins tomorrow."

Kay slid her gaze to the woman next to her.

Ariana fidgeted with her coffee cup. "Yes. Of course. Tulum. I've always wanted to see the ruins."

Millie was dying to ask her if it had anything to do with her father's archaeological background, but she held her tongue, not wanting to tip her hand.

"What time should we leave?" Millie had a sneaking suspicion that Christopher was part of the plan.

"The shuttle leaves at 9:45 so I think if we are off the ship by 9:15 we'll have plenty of time."

Millie snuck a glance at Kay who gave her a brief nod, as if to say. "She won't escape this time."

Ariana wasn't scheduled to perform that evening. The women finished their dessert and Ariana informed them that she wanted to watch the headliner in the theater.

Millie, who wanted to stop by the bridge, parted ways with Ariana and Kay outside the dining room.

She missed Scout...and the captain. She used her keycard to let herself inside the bridge.

The lights were low and the room was quiet except for the faint hum of the computers. Captain Armati was standing in front of the windows. She cleared her throat as she entered the room.

The captain swung around. His eyes lit up and a slow smile crept across his face. "Millie. What a pleasant surprise."

"I...I hope I'm not interrupting."

The captain shoved his hands in the front pockets of his jacket. "No. Not at all. Captain Vitale and Ingrid have gone out for a bite to eat."

He went on. "Have you eaten?"

She nodded. "Yes. I had dinner with my new sidekick, Ariana."

"How is that going?"

Millie rubbed the back of her neck as she remembered the uncomfortable cot. "Let's just say I can't wait to dock in Miami."

He waved an arm toward his private apartment. "Do you have a minute to say hello to Scout? I'm sure he would love to see you."

"Yes. Please. If you don't mind."

She followed the captain down the small hall and waited while he entered the access code on the door. The familiar beep sounded. The captain pressed down on the handle and the door swung open.

Scout was waiting on the other side and when he spotted Millie, he promptly tried to climb her leg. She lifted him in her arms and he began to lick her face, her neck, her ear.

"I can't leave the bridge unattended," he told her, "but you can bring Scout out here if you want to visit for a moment."

Millie trailed along behind and followed him to the center of the room and over to the computer console. She stood next to him and stared at the screen. In the center of the screen was a large round picture. Several charts and graphs dotted the outer edge.

She couldn't make heads or tails of the center circle or any of the charts that surrounded it.

"The views through the window are much more interesting," he said.

Millie set Scout on the floor and wandered over to the window. She stared out at the dark ocean. Thick clouds filled the sky and blotted out the stars. Only a small sliver of moon broke through the clouds and provided a small beam of light that slithered across the water.

"I have one more week and then I will be off on my break," he said.

Millie had almost forgotten. With all the excitement and drama surrounding Ariana, she hadn't had much time to think about anything else.

Scout darted across the room when he heard someone at the outer door. "Will Scout go with you?"

He nodded. "Yes. My daughter Fiona is anxious to see him."

Ingrid Kozlov stepped inside the bridge and closed the door behind her.

Captain turned his attention to her. "Good evening Ingrid. I trust you enjoyed your dinner."

"Yes, captain." She smiled at the captain and glared at Millie.

"I should get back to Ariana." Millie told him.

Captain walked her to the door and stepped outside, out of Ingrid's hearing range. "Are you going ashore in Cozumel tomorrow?"

"Yes. Ariana is determined to see the Mayan ruins," she said.

He nodded. "They are magnificent. Perhaps next time we are in port, you will allow me to show you around?"

Millie turned a tint of pink. "I-I would like that. A lot."

"Good," he nodded in approval. "Me, too. I would like that a lot."

He turned to go. "Scout and I...we will miss you."

The captain turned and headed back inside, silently closing the door behind him.

Millie stared at the door for a long moment, wondering if she had somehow gotten water in her ears or if she had heard the captain correctly.

Certain that she had heard him right, Millie pivoted on her heel and floated off down the hall. If not for Ariana and her antics, today would have been a near perfect day!

Chapter 11

The next morning, Millie awoke to the sound of a dull thud coming from somewhere close by. It took her several moments to figure out where she was. When she shifted in the bed, her bones ached and her neck refused to turn.

The dull thud was coming from the bathroom. She glanced over at Ariana's empty bed.

Millie flung the covers back and swung her legs over the side as she shuffled over to the light switch on the wall. Dim light lit illuminated the area over the makeup counter.

Millie leaned in for a closer inspection of her reflection. She had slept better last night than the night before but she would be more than ready to have this adventure with Ariana end.

Millie picked up her watch and squinted at the face. She had an hour before she had to meet Annette and Cat near the exit.

Millie glanced at the bathroom door and then at the pair of slacks she had been wearing the day before. She reached inside the pocket and pulled out the small tracking chip.

Ariana's fanny pack was sitting on the desk. Millie quickly unzipped the pack and rifled through the contents. If Ariana had hidden something inside, it was long gone!

Millie flipped the pack over, searching for some sort of spot to hide the tiny device.

Millie's eyes darted to the door when she heard Ariana start to hum. She needed to hurry!

She stuck her hand inside the bag and her fingers fumbled with a small, narrow liner in the very bottom of the pack.

She picked up the chip and quickly shoved it as far back in the liner as she could. When the chip was safely in place, Millie shoved Ariana's cell phone, lip balm and small wallet back inside.

As soon as she zipped it shut and dropped it on the counter, the door to the bathroom flung open.

Millie jerked upright and did the first thing that came to mind: clutched her stomach. "Oh, it's a good thing you're done." She darted past Ariana, grabbed the door handle and disappeared inside as she pulled the door closed behind her. She leaned against the door and closed her eyes. That had been a close call!

Millie quickly showered and changed into the clean clothes she had brought with her the night before. She dried her hair, smoothed it back into a tight ponytail and then wrapped it into a loose bun.

The girls would have just enough time to run up to the breakfast buffet for a cup of coffee and quick bite to eat before they had to get off.

The balcony door was open when Millie emerged. Millie's heart sank as she dropped her dirty clothes on the end of the cot.

The first thing she noticed was that the room was empty. The second thing she noticed was that Ariana's fanny pack was gone...

Millie made her way over to the balcony but she knew without even looking outside that Ariana wouldn't be there. She was right. The balcony was empty.

She stepped over to Kay's cabin door and knocked. When no one answered, she knocked harder. There was still no answer.

Millie grabbed the door handle and slowly turned. The door wasn't locked. She pushed the door open and peeked inside. A small sliver of light crept in through the open door and illuminated the small bed, which was empty.

Both women were gone!

Millie grabbed her backpack, dropped her lanyard around her neck and headed for the door.

On her way to the gangway, she stopped by the buffet for a quick cup of coffee, some bacon, eggs and toast. She might as well go out with a full stomach since she had a feeling that her day would be spent chasing after Ariana.

She was relieved that Annette and Cat would be with her to help her track the woman down. Two could play that game!

After she finished her breakfast, she headed to the exit and waited off to one side. Annette and Cat were right on time. "Where's Ariana?" Cat asked.

"She snuck off," Millie said.

"You don't look too concerned," Annette commented.

"I'm not. She took off with her fanny pack which just so happens to have your tracking device hidden in the bottom." She grinned.

Annette reached back and patted her backpack. "She won't get far."

The women started to make their way across the docking area to a tender boat nearby. "I'm pretty sure she intends to visit the Mayan ruins so if we head in that direction, we won't be far behind her."

They boarded the tender for the short ride across the choppy water. Millie mulled over everything she knew. Ariana – and Christopher – were searching for something. Had they found it? What had been in Ariana's fanny pack?

Was Kay in on it? She hadn't seemed to be. In fact, the woman seemed downright ticked off when Ariana and Millie had gone cave tubing without her.

What about Pierre? Where did he fit in? Then there was the guy named Firkin that Christopher and Ariana pointed out yesterday.

Millie was beginning to feel as if someone had dropped her right in the middle of a James Bond movie and she was the only one who had no idea what was going on.

When the shuttle docked on the other side, the girls wandered through the downtown tourist strip. Gift shops lined the street, along with coffee shops and cafes. It was a colorful, festive area and it looked as if it was a popular spot to vacation. She wondered if Captain Armati had ever been there.

Several taxis lined the street and the girls headed to the one near the end. Annette leaned down and poked her head inside the open passenger window. "Tulum?"

The driver nodded. "I can take you to Tulum."

The girls climbed in the taxi with Annette riding shotgun. Cat and Millie sat in the back seat. The interior of the cab was hot and sticky. Either the taxi's air conditioning didn't work or the taxi was so old, it had been built before AC was considered standard equipment.

The car bumped along the road and over several potholes. Millie wondered if the taxi had shocks as it jostled her insides and she began to feel queasy.

The driver was entertaining and made small talk during the ride. "You are from the ship?"

"Yes," Annette said. "We work on the ship."

"Ah, I see. You like working on the ship?"

"It's exciting," Millie mumbled.

As they drove down the back roads, the driver pointed out various attractions along the way. One in particular caught Millie's eye. The taxi driver described it as a tropical oasis. It was a tourist resort that offered all you could eat and drink. They also had a long list of water activities: snorkeling, kayaking, canoeing, inflatable water toys.

Millie stared at the entrance as they passed by. "We should try that place next time we're here."

The driver lifted his hand and rubbed his thumb and index finger together. "It cost a lot of money."

"Never mind," Millie said.

Annette reached inside her backpack and pulled out her cell phone. She pressed several buttons and squinted at the screen. "Nothing on the tracking device yet. We must be too far away."

She shoved the phone inside her backpack and zipped it shut.

The taxi veered off the road and onto a side street that was in even worse condition than the road they had just been on. The heat and bouncing was getting to Millie. "Can you roll down the back window?"

The driver nodded. "The handle. It is on the door."

Millie shifted her gaze to inspect the door next to her. Sure enough, it was a crank window. She turned the handle and rolled the window down. A blast of hot, tropical air rushed in. It was better, but not much.

The taxi came to an abrupt halt in front of thick line of foliage. "We are here," he announced.

Cat leaned forward and stared out the window. "This is Tulum?"

The driver nodded. "On the other side of that bush, you will see a large building with shops. Walk past the shops and you will find the entrance to the ruins."

Millie pulled some bills from her purse and handed $20 to the driver. "Is this enough?"

He nodded. "Si. Thank you. Do you want me to pick you up later?"

Cat frowned. They hadn't thought about how they would get back to the ship! "We're not sure how long. Are taxis waiting here to take visitors back?"

"Si. But they can be few and far between."

Millie frowned. On the one hand, she wasn't sure how long it would take to track down Ariana. Then again, she didn't want to get stuck out here in the middle of nowhere and risk missing the ship.

She glanced at her watch. They had all day. The ship wasn't scheduled to leave until 5:00 p.m. and it was only 10:30 in the morning. "We'll just have to take our chances."

Millie's gut warned her that statement would come back to haunt her...

***

The girls wandered past the bushes and just as the driver had said, there was a clearing behind it. In the clearing was a long, low building with a galvanized steel roof. Inside the building were rows of small booths. The girls bypassed the booths and made their way over to the entrance to Tulum.

Annette pulled her phone from her purse and studied the screen. "Still nothing. No...wait! I see a small blip on the screen."

She waved them forward. "Let's go!"

The girls jogged to the entrance, a covered pavilion. Annette paid the entrance fee and the trio waited while a uniformed security guard checked their bags.

Finally, they made it through the security checkpoint and faced the massive, ancient structure.

A tall, stone wall surrounded the ruins. The tippy tops of several ruins were visible over the top of the wall. Millie hoped they would have a little time to explore the ruins but knew her first priority was to track Ariana, or whoever the woman was, down.

There were two entrances: one was a side entrance. A steep set of steps ran up the side of the fortress wall and disappeared along the tree line. The second entrance was a large set of double doors near the center of the wall. The girls opted for the path of least resistance and headed for the main entrance.

Inside the gate were several dirt paths that shot out in different directions. The paths were dotted with rough rocks and smooth stones.

Millie gazed around in awe. It was as if she had stepped back in time. There were no gift shops, no paved walkways or grassy areas with cozy park benches.

The Mayan ruins were impressive; the hand-hewn structures depicted different scenes. The structures were all different levels. Each started with a large, square base and on top of the base was another, smaller square.

At the very top of the structures were square blocks. The blocks on top were roughly the size of a small shed. The centers of the blocks had been carved out. Millie could see straight through the center and daylight on the other side.

She stepped close to one. Carved on the outside was a half-dragon, half-human. On the upper half of the body were two hairy hands that reached toward a tree. The bottom half of the body had a tail and on the tail was a turtle.

Millie shuffled to the side. The second carving was a large skull, the teeth clearly visible. On both sides of the skull were smaller skulls, tilted at various angles.

A twinge of fear crept up Millie's spine. This place was creepy in broad daylight. She couldn't imagine what it would be like in the dead of the night!

Annette paid little attention to the ruins. Instead, she focused on her phone. "The signal is getting stronger. This way!"

She didn't wait for an answer as she scurried down a dirt path toward the back of the ruins. Cat and Millie picked up the pace and followed behind.

When they reached the outer ruins, Annette paused to study the front of her phone.

Millie glanced around. The girls were standing near the edge of a cliff. Off to one side was a set of steep steps that led down to a beach below. Several people, who looked more like ants, lounged on the beach or frolicked in the water.

Annette pointed to the beach area below. "It looks like we'll have to go that way."

The girls descended the steps and stopped near the water's edge. The sun was high in the sky and Annette had to shield her screen with her hand to keep a visual. She pointed to the right. "That way."

Millie frowned. The small beach area ended near a line of thick foliage. All she could see was a small footpath that led straight into the jungle!

"A-are you sure?" she said.

"I dunno about this," Cat argued. This was a bona fide jungle. People disappeared in jungles, never to be seen again!

Annette ignored their hesitation and started toward the dense foliage. It left Cat and Millie little choice but to follow behind.

Chapter 12

Millie was the last to step onto the narrow path and enter the dense jungle. Cat swatted at a thick clump of tall bushes. One of the large palm fronds whipped backward and smacked Millie in the face.

Millie reared back as sticky silk from a spider web stuck to her cheek. "Eek!" she shrieked.

"What?" Annette spun around.

Millie shivered. "Spider webs." Her eyes traveled above her as she studied the thick vines and limbs high overhead.

Moments later, they reached a fork in the path. Annette paused. "This way." She pointed to the left.

Cat, the voice of reason, spoke up. "What if we get lost?"

"Not possible." Annette shook her head. "The GPS on my phone will get us out of here."

"Unless the battery dies," Millie pointed out.

"True," Annette agreed. "Hey! I think we're getting close!"

The trio stumbled along through the jungle. The mosquitos were thick and Millie began a steady pattern of slap, walk, slap, walk.

Cat giggled. "You sound like you're practicing for a one man band."

"The mosquitos are eating me alive," Millie moaned.

"Something is attracting them. Did you eat a banana for breakfast?"

Millie frowned. "Yeah. What's that got to do with anything?"

Annette nodded knowingly. "Although it's supposedly an old wives' tale, I think it's the B12 in the banana. It's like a magnet for mosquitoes."

Just Millie's luck! How was she to know she would be traipsing through a rainforest?

Annette stopped abruptly. "Shh! I hear something."

The girls stopped in their tracks. The only thing Millie could hear was the chatter of jungle creatures. Probably a killer ape...

Annette took a step forward. Cat and Millie were close behind.

Annette leaned forward, grasped the edge of a thick frond and slowly pushed it aside. Cat and Millie peered over her shoulder and gazed into a clearing. The sight in front of them made Millie's heart skip a beat.

Cat's hand flew to her mouth.

There, lying on a large, stone slab was Ariana, her body blood red. Leaning over the top of her was Kay!

***

Annette charged full speed ahead.

Cat hovered near the edge.

Millie froze. The hair on the back of her neck stood on end. She felt someone staring at her. She turned her head slowly to the side.

Through the vines and the bushes, Millie could make out a pair of sharp blue eyes that pierced into hers. It was man and his face was painted green, which closely matched the leaves that surrounded him.

"No!" he hissed at the girls in an attempt to stop them. But it was too late. Annette darted into the clearing and tackled Kay to the ground.

Ariana bolted upright on the slab. "What is going on?" she demanded.

Annette quickly pinned Kay's shoulders to the damp earth. "We're here to rescue you!" she said breathlessly.

The man in the bush gave Millie a warning look before he melted back into the jungle. Had he been trying to rescue Ariana...or was he following the girls?

Millie didn't have time to dwell on that as she raced across the opening to help Ariana. When she got close to the cement slab, she realized that it wasn't blood covering Ariana, but rather a deep, rich clay. Deep cracks in the clay had opened up where sections had dried.

Kay struggled to escape Annette's ironclad grip. "Let me go!"

Annette lifted her leg as she released her hold on Kay and jumped to her feet. "We thought Ariana's life was in danger."

Cat pointed to the slab of cement. "What is that?" It looked like some sort of sacrificial platform built by the ancient Mayans.

Ariana wiped a glob of the clay-like substance off her cheek. "I read online the soil was good for my skin so Kay and I hiked back here to check it out." She pointed up. "Once we slathered a bunch on, I laid on this rock so the creepy crawlies wouldn't get me. The light through the trees helped dry the clay."

Millie had had it up to her eyeballs with Ariana's antics. She reached out and grabbed ahold of her arm. The mud squished between her fingers. "You've gone too far this time," she warned. "I think a just punishment would be for you to leave the goop on your body until you get back to the ship. It ought to be nice and ripe by then!"

Never mind that no taxi driver in his right mind would let her climb into his cab covered in mud. Still, at the very least, Ariana would have to suffer until they reached civilization.

Ariana yanked her arm her arm from Millie's grasp. "I don't think so," she snarled.

"C'mon." Ariana motioned to Kay and grabbed her fanny pack propped up against the slab. The two women disappeared into the dense jungle.

Millie made a move to follow behind since she wasn't even close to being finished with Ariana, but Cat wisely grabbed her hand and stopped her. "You better just let her go and cool off."

Millie paused. Cat was right. There was no sense in making it even worse. She took a deep breath and closed her eyes. "You're right."

The girls followed behind Kay and Ariana as they began to retrace their steps through the rainforest. They walked for several minutes in silence. Millie was still steamed as she stomped along, sandwiched between Annette in the front and Cat in the rear.

When they got to the fork in the path, Annette paused. "Should we go right or left?"

Millie frowned. "Right?" she guessed.

"What does the GPS say?" Cat asked.

Annette slowly shook her head. "The battery is getting low and I can't see the signal."

Wouldn't that be just their luck to get lost in the jungle? Millie began to giggle.

The irony of the situation struck Cat's funny bone and she burst out laughing. "Oh my gosh! We were supposed to be the rescuers and now look at us."

Even Annette grinned. "If we're lucky, Ariana is lost, too."

She grew somber as she glanced up at the sky. It had to be getting close to mid-afternoon. They would have to figure out how to get out of the jungle soon.

Daylight would eventually fade and she didn't want to be wandering around the jungle in the dark. Not only that, they would miss the boat...or in this case, the ship.

The girls, faced with the gravity of the situation, turned in the direction that two of the three had agreed was the right way. They soon discovered it was not the right way and attempted to backtrack before heading in the opposite direction.

Half an hour later, Millie recognized a large boulder that was off to one side. The boulder had an odd marking on top. She stopped abruptly. "We've been by here already."

Cat looked at the rock and frowned. "You're right."

They both turned to Annette. "Now what?"

By now, another hour had passed. Millie glanced at her watch. It was 3:40. The ship was leaving at 5:00. She quickly calculated in her head that between the taxi ride, the walk through town and the shuttle boat ride, it would take a good hour to make it back to the ship! They had twenty minutes to get out of the jungle or chance Siren of the Seas leaving them behind!

Millie pushed through the brush as she frantically searched for a way back. She caught a glimpse of water through the thick brush. "This way!"

The girls snaked their way through the overgrown foliage as they made their way to the sandy shoreline nearby.

"If we follow along the beach, we should end up back near Tulum," Millie theorized.

They were in a race against time as they picked up the pace and began to run along the water line.

Soon, the steps leading to the Tulum ruins were in sight. Millie could have cried with joy but she didn't have time.

The girls bolted up the stairs and ran through the center of the ruins.

Millie took a quick glance at the ancient structures...so much for being able to tour the ruins!

They darted through the exit and across the parking lot.

Annette spied one lone taxi near the curb. With a sudden burst of energy, she lurched forward and began to pound on the trunk of the vehicle as it started to pull away.

The driver, seeing a crazy old woman in his rearview mirror, stomped on the brakes.

Annette slammed into the rear of the bumper and doubled over "Umpf!"

Millie raced over to check to see if she was all right.

Cat raced to the driver's side of the taxi. "We need to get to the port right away."

She glanced inside the taxi. There were already two occupants. The girls would have to squeeze in tight to fit.

The driver nodded his head and motioned for them to climb in.

Annette got in first.

"Are you okay?" Cat asked anxiously.

Annette nodded, but she was still holding her stomach. "Just got the wind knocked out of me. I'm fine."

She turned to the driver. "We'll pay you double if you get us back to the port by 4:30." She glanced at the clock on the dashboard. It was 4:15.

He shook his head. "No senorita. It will be at least 4:40, even if I push the pedal to the metal the entire way."

Millie swallowed the lump in her throat. The only thing they could do was pray.

The wide-eyed young couple in the taxi turned to Millie. "Do you think we'll miss the ship?" the woman whispered.

Cat, who sat next to the young girl, sighed. "I sure hope not."

True to his word, the driver stomped on the gas and the car raced down the road. The back end wobbled and wiggled and Millie prayed the wheels weren't about to fall off.

She closed her eyes. "Dear Lord. Please get us back to the port safely. Please let us make it in time so that we don't have to swim home."

Her eyes jerked open when the driver slammed on the brakes and the car skidded sideways. A horse and buggy had pulled into their path and the front of the car was mere inches from the rear of the carriage.

The buggy driver, his eyes filled with terror, reined the horses off to the side to let the taxi veer around them.

The taxi driver wiped the sweat from his brow. "That was close!"

Moments later, the taxi pulled as close to the dock and shuttle boat as possible. Annette threw a handful of bills at the driver. Three of the four doors burst open and the five occupants dashed out of the cab and made a run for the shuttle boat.

The boat had just lifted the ropes from around the dock post and started to drift away from the dock.

Cat cupped her hands to her mouth. "Wait!" she screamed in desperation. The five of them stampeded to the dock and held their breath as the ship's captain gazed at them, as if deciding whether to come back.

Millie could see he was torn. He must have decided that five passengers equaled five fares he wouldn't otherwise collect so he eased the boat back to the slip and motioned them to climb aboard.

The crew didn't tie the boat up but rather helped each of them navigate the slippery steps.

Millie let out a sigh of relief when they were safely onboard and heading across open water.

She began to feel better about their dilemma until Annette groaned. "Oh no! Look at that!"

Millie gazed across the water toward Siren of the Seas. Thick smoke poured from ship's funnels. Millie had watched the ship leave port many times and judging by the scurrying crew near the edge of the dock, she knew they were almost out of time. She glanced down at her watch: 5:01 p.m.

"It-it's too late, isn't it?" Annette asked.

Cat covered her eyes and shook her head. "Please tell me it isn't too late."

"It isn't too late," Millie said.

Cat's head lifted. "You mean we still have time to make it?"

"No. I was just saying what you told me to say," Millie answered.

Annette reached over and whacked her leg. "That's not funny!"

The young couple that had now joined them on their adventure turned to Millie. "*Will* the ship leave us behind?"

Millie gazed at the ship and noticed the crew had disappeared. Water churned near the back of the boat, which meant only one thing: the propellers were moving...moving the ship away from the dock. "I believe they have."

All eyes turned to the ship...their ship as it drifted away from the massive concrete dock.

By now, the small ferry was halfway across the inlet and nearing the outer edges of the cruise ship dock. Millie was desperate and did the only thing she could think to do. She plucked her cell phone from her backpack and dialed Captain Armati's cell phone number.

Chapter 13

Millie tried to sound casual when Captain Armati answered. "Millie! Where are you?"

"Sitting in a shuttle boat watching Siren of the Seas leave me behind."

"Us!" Cat piped up.

"Us," she corrected herself. "Annette, Cat, me, plus two young passengers."

"How," he started to ask and then stopped. "Forget I asked."

He let out a long sigh and Millie cringed inwardly. "I tried to stall for more time but port authorities are waiting to dock another ship and we had to pull anchor," he explained.

He went on. "You have two choices. You can go back to shore and we can arrange for flights back to Miami since we don't have another port stop."

Millie wasn't keen on that choice. "What is my other option?"

"You can ask the shuttle captain to bring you out to the ship and try to board in open water."

Millie frowned. In her opinion, they didn't have a choice. She glanced at the young couple. They appeared to be in good health and agile. She was certain they would have a good shot at boarding the ship.

"Let's try it," Millie said.

"Would you like to run it by the others first?" he asked.

Millie shook her head, as if the captain could see her through the phone. "They don't have to try it but I'm gonna give it a go."

Captain Armati instructed her to have the shuttle boat bring them to the starboard side where crew would be waiting. Millie thanked the captain, and silently vowed to do that in person once they were safely back onboard.

Millie hung up the phone, shoved it in her pocket and turned to the small ferryboat captain. "Can you pull up to the ship's starboard side? We're going to try to board in open water."

The captain started to shake his head but changed his mind. "Yes. We will try, although I have never done this before," he admitted.

With those words of encouragement, Millie turned to the others. "We have two choices. Turn around and head back to shore where we will have to book a flight back to Miami. Our second choice, and the one I am willing to try, is to have the shuttle ease up next to Siren of the Seas and board boat-to-boat."

The young couple nodded. They were all in.

"Sounds like a plan." Annette clasped her hands together.

Cat was the only one on the fence. "I don't know about this..."

"I'll go first since it was my idea," Millie offered.

They agreed that Millie would be the first to try, followed by Annette. After Annette, the young girl and young man. Cat would be the last in line.

The shuttle headed toward the large cruise ship and the starboard side. Millie could see that the crew had already opened the side entrance.

Millie's gaze wandered to the windows of the bridge. She thought she saw Captain Armati and Captain Vitale as they stood near the bridge's windows and watched.

She focused her attention on the open door and caught a glimpse of Andy hovering in the background. Last but not least, she lifted her eyes to the ship's upper railings. "We have an audience," she muttered.

Cruise ship passengers crowded along the railings to watch. Some were holding cameras, eager to capture the unorthodox boarding on video.

Annette stood near the edge of the small rail and waved. "We're gonna be famous," she joked.

"More like infamous," Cat shot back.

"We'll never live this down," Millie predicted.

The small shuttle stopped mere inches from the side of the hulking cruise ship. One of the shuttle crew tossed two thick ropes up to the crew of Siren of the Seas.

The workers onboard the massive ship tied the ropes to metal hooks on either side of the door.

One of the crew dropped a rope ladder off the side of the cruise ship, anchoring the center of the ladder to a hook in the floor of the ship.

The shuttle captain turned. "Who will go first?"

Millie pointed to herself. "Me." She climbed up on the fiberglass top and shuffled to the edge as she reached for the ladder.

Two of the workers fought to steady her as the smaller boat bobbed up and down between waves. Millie would have to time it just right so that the small shuttle crested a wave at the same time she reached for a rung of the ladder.

Millie sucked in her breath and reached for the rungs. Her fingertips touched the metal but the wave dropped too quickly.

She began to lose her balance as she started to tip forward. Her arms flailed wildly in the air. "I'm going over!"

The passengers gasped in horror.

The shuttle crew grabbed her arms and pulled her back, just in time.

Millie closed her eyes and whispered a quick prayer as she waited for the next wave. Her heart pounded as the wave lifted the small boat, bringing her within inches of the ladder.

Millie lunged forward as she reached out with both hands. She clamped onto the metal rung and held on for dear life.

Her feet dangled beneath her as she hung suspended in mid-air for just a moment.

She desperately kicked her feet against the side of the ship until her foot made contact with the rung. She quickly brought her second foot to the rung.

With both hands and feet securely on the rungs, Millie climbed the ladder to the opening in the side of the ship. When she reached the open door, two strong hands reached down, grasped her upper arms and dragged her inside where she flopped face down on the metal floor.

Echoes of rejoicing voices filled the air as Millie kissed the floor and jumped to her feet triumphantly.

She hugged both of her rescuers, and turned back once to give the other four hovering near the shuttle's rail the thumbs up. Her legs shook as she wobbled over to Andy.

Andy hugged Millie tight then let her go. You'll do anything for attention," he teased.

Millie opened her mouth to give him some lip but he held up a hand. "Just kidding."

Millie turned her attention to the open door. Annette was next. Millie couldn't see what was happening outside but judging by the gasps and groans from the crew, she had a feeling that Annette had almost gone over, too.

When Millie caught a glimpse of the top of Annette's head, she released the breath she'd been holding.

The crew grabbed Annette's arms and hoisted her onto solid ground where she landed in exactly the same spot that Millie had – face down.

Millie burst out laughing when Annette kissed the metal floor, too.

Annette thanked her rescuers, lifted both hands and gave two thumbs up to the three remaining passengers waiting to board.

She made her way over to Millie and Andy. "I'm not sure I want to try that again. It gives me a greater appreciation for the gangway."

Millie couldn't agree more.

The trio turned their attention to the open doorway. There were no gasps or moans from the crew and soon, the young woman who had been on board the shuttle was in view.

The crew lifted her up but she was more agile than Annette and Millie and managed to land on her feet. The girls clapped their hands and she wandered over to join them.

Millie gave her a quick hug. "Good job."

The girl grinned. "That was kinda fun!"

The young man was next and the crew quickly lifted him to safety where he joined the others.

Millie took a quick peek behind her. Dave Patterson had joined the growing crowd and he winked when he caught Millie's eye.

The only person left was Cat and Millie was concerned. She had seemed anxious about boarding in open water and Millie feared she might chicken out.

When the crew began to motion to her down below, Millie knew they were in trouble. She could just envision poor Cat frozen with fear.

Millie made her way over to the open door and stood next to one of the rescue crew. She grabbed hold of a side handle and leaned over the edge. The first thing she noticed was the panicked look on her friend's face. Their eyes locked.

"You can do it," Millie said. She wasn't sure Cat could hear her.

Cat started to shake her head.

Millie, determined to get Cat on board the ship safe and sound, cupped her hands around her mouth and yelled, "Yes. You can!"

Cat closed her eyes for a second. She opened her eyes and nodded.

She was finally going to give it a try!

Millie sucked in a breath as she watched Cat ease onto the fiberglass top. The shuttle crew held her steady as they waited for the wave to crest.

Cat reached out, as if to grab the ladder rung but quickly snatched her hand back.

"You can do it!" Millie shouted down.

Cat locked eyes with Millie once again.

Millie held her breath and waited for the next wave.

With a leap of faith, Cat lunged for the ladder and kicked her feet in front of her. One hand gripped the ladder and one foot caught the rung. She swayed back and forth for a brief second before her other hand clawed at the rung and grabbed hold of the metal handle.

When her other foot safely landed on the rung, the crowd cheered wildly. Cat, blinded by fear, didn't hear them as she scrambled up the ladder at record speed.

The crew was gentler with Cat and she landed on her feet. When they released their grip, she began to sway.

Millie reached over, put an arm around her waist and flung her other arm around her friend's neck. "You did it!" Millie rejoiced.

"I was staring death in the face," Cat gasped dramatically.

"You were not!" Millie argued.

The young couple waited off to the side and when Annette noticed them standing there, she motioned them over. "Good job, you two."

The young man grinned. "We were just talking. We decided if we ever cruise again, we want to come back on Siren of the Seas and hang out with you three."

Andy snorted. "You don't know what you're getting yourselves into," he warned.

Millie thanked the crew once again and turned to the girls. "I better get cleaned up." She knew she smelled to high heaven from sweat, not to mention dirt and the clay that Ariana had coated on her body.

Her first order of business was to shower and then stop by the bridge to thank the captain in person for waiting for them. Her second order of business was to track down Ariana!

Chapter 14

Millie took a long, leisurely shower, rejoicing in the fact that she was no longer lost in the middle of the rainforest or still in Mexico, trying to find a flight back to Miami.

She emerged from the shower squeaky clean and smelling like a rose, thanks to the new rose scented body wash she had just purchased.

Millie's cabin was quiet and cool and tears stung the back of her eyes as she realized how much she missed her cozy little home.

She was tired of traipsing after Ariana, if that was even her name. She was tired of sleeping on a cot and last but not least, she was tired of being led on wild goose chases. Millie's only consolation was there were no more port stops and Ariana could only go so far!

Millie changed into a work uniform, pulled her damp hair into a ponytail and then clipped it in place with a plastic hair clip before she dropped her lanyard around her neck and headed for the door.

Millie tapped on the outer door of the bridge before she let herself in using her key card. Captain Armati and Captain Vitale stood in the center of the room, studying the monitor.

Ingrid was off to one side peering at a smaller screen.

The men looked up as she approached.

Millie's face turned a deep shade of crimson as they began to clap their hands. "Well done, Millie," Captain Vitale grinned.

Captain Armati shook his head. "Millie...what are we going to do with you?"

"It's not only me," she argued.

"True," he agreed. "I'll give you that." He changed the subject. "Would you like to say hello to Scout?"

Millie nodded then followed him down the small hall to his apartment. The door was ajar and he pushed to open it wide.

Scout was near the slider looking out. When he saw Millie, he shot to his feet and raced across the room.

Millie picked him up and for the second time that day, her throat swelled and she blinked back tears. *Pull yourself together*...she silently scolded herself.

The captain crossed his arms and watched the happy reunion. "We miss you," he simply said.

She set Scout on the floor and a lone tear trailed down Millie's cheek. "I-I..."

The captain reached out and wrapped his arms around Millie, pulling her close. "It will be all right," he whispered in her hair.

A swirl of emotions filled Millie. Her heart began to pound and her pulse quickened. Captain...Nic...smelled nice and felt even better.

For a moment, she allowed herself the luxury of having a man touch her again...and it felt wonderful.

When he finally pulled away, he gazed into her eyes.

The captain...Nic...slowly lowered his head. His lips brushed against hers in a slow, seductive kiss.

Millie closed her eyes.

Tap, tap. Her eyes flew open. Someone was knocking on the door!

The moment was lost. The captain pulled back and stared down at her apologetically. "I must answer that," he said.

Millie nodded. "Of course."

The captain stepped over to the door and pulled it open. It was Ingrid. "I am sorry, but a crew member from the engine room is on the phone." Her steely gaze slid to Millie as she smirked at her in triumph. It was as if somehow Ingrid knew!

Millie followed the captain out, careful to leave poor Scout behind. "I'll be back soon," she promised as she closed the door behind her.

The captain had already picked up the phone on the far wall and was in deep conversation.

Captain Vitale stood near the windows and Millie gave a small wave as she headed to the exit.

Millie silently opened the door and then quietly closed it behind her. She pressed her hands to her cheeks as she headed down the stairs. The kiss had left her whole body tingling. It had been so long since a man had kissed her, she had almost forgotten what it felt like!

The warm and fuzzy feeling lasted until Millie reached the upper level theater – and Ariana's suite.

Millie tapped on the outer door and waited. Kay opened the door, took one look at Millie's expression and eased past her. "I was just leaving." She hustled across the floor and disappeared through the theater exit. Kay was just as much to blame, at least in Millie's mind.

Millie stepped inside the suite where she found Ariana lounging on the sofa, a bag of potato chips next to her. She plucked one of the salty snacks from the bag and popped it into her mouth. "You look fit to be tied," she observed.

Millie shuffled over to the cot and plopped down on the edge. "It has been a long day, thanks to you."

Ariana reached her hand inside the bag for another chip and Millie noticed the scar on her wrist.

Millie impulsively licked her index finger, reached over and rubbed it across Ariana's scar. The "scar" began to smear.

Ariana pulled her arm away. "What are you doing?"

Millie cocked her head. "Who are you?"

"Ariana Teliar."

"No. You're not." Millie pointed to the smeared scar. "The real Ariana Teliar/Gatwick has a birthmark on her wrist and I'm pretty sure it's permanent, unlike your fake scar. Start again. Who are you?"

Ariana slid off the couch and waved Millie to the balcony. "Outside."

Millie started to follow Ariana outside when her gaze fell on the fanny pack lying on the small end table. "First things first."

She unzipped the fanny pack, reached inside and plucked out Annette's tracking device.

Ariana raised a brow. "Nice," she complimented. "I wondered how you found me."

The women walked out onto the balcony and Ariana closed the door behind them. "The room may be bugged," she explained.

Millie nodded. True. Nothing would surprise her at this point.

Ariana stepped over to the balcony and placed her elbows on the rail. The ocean breeze lifted wisps of blonde hair and tossed them across her face.

"Before I start my story, I just want to say kudos to you for the brave boarding earlier. You would make a great undercover agent." She narrowed her eyes. "In fact, you would make an excellent undercover agent. No one would ever suspect you."

"Thanks," Millie replied grudgingly. "So what's the story? Who are you?"

"Danielle Kneldon, part time archaeologist, full time undercover agent." She placed one arm across her waist and the other behind her back as she lowered into a mock bow. "At your service."

"Danielle. So Jacob Gatwick hired you to pretend to be his daughter?"

"Correct," Danielle aka Ariana agreed.

"He also hired you to track something down in the jungles, namely Costa Maya. That's why Christopher and you snuck off during the cave tubing."

Danielle nodded. "Yep. Two for two."

"Did you find what you were after?" Millie asked.

Danielle raised a brow. "Perhaps."

Millie believed that she had but didn't press the issue. "Does anyone on board, other than me, know that you are not the real Ariana Teliar / Gatwick?"

Danielle shook her head. "Nope. None of them had ever seen Ariana up close, not even

Kay, and that was one of the reasons Mr. Gatwick chose me."

Millie pointed at her arm. "Except for the scar."

"Except for the scar," Danielle agreed. "Someone is trying to kill Ariana...or in this case, me."

"Kay or Pierre?" Millie probed. "Or possibly even Christopher?"

Danielle shrugged. "I haven't ruled anyone out."

Millie grew silent as she stared out at the water. "Why would you run off to the jungle with someone who may be trying to take you out?"

Danielle smiled wickedly. "Oh, Millie...I had such high hopes for you," she teased. "Because I was trying to flush out the killer, which might have worked if you hadn't burst on the scene trying to rescue me." She patted Millie's hand. "Thanks for that."

"You could've been killed!" Millie pointed out.

Danielle shrugged. "I can handle myself."

Millie paused, in deep thought as she mulled over what Ariana...Danielle had just told her. "What about the Firkin guy from yesterday?"

"Christopher told me he isn't onboard the ship, but then I can't trust Christopher so maybe he's lying and Firkin is onboard."

Millie thought back to the first day Danielle had boarded. She remembered poor Miguel, found dead on the balcony. "Miguel, the security guard...his death is somehow linked to you."

Danielle tapped the rail with her fingernail. "I think that whoever is trying to kill Ariana...me, tried to smuggle a weapon, probably a handgun, on board and when Miguel discovered the weapon, the perpetrator killed him and then left his body on my balcony as a warning."

Millie frowned. Whoever this was meant business. She glanced at Danielle from the corner of her eye. The young woman seemed to take it all in stride…

Danielle began to scratch the top of her arms. "Oh my gosh! I don't know what was in that mud today but my skin is starting to itch like crazy!" she moaned.

Millie grabbed Ariana's arm and turned it over. It was loaded with tiny red welts. "It looks as if you might have had a run in with a colony of fire ants," Millie chuckled. "Serves you right!"

"I'm sorry for all the trouble I've caused." Danielle turned to head back inside. "In a couple more days I'll be off the ship and out of your hair," she promised.

Millie started to follow behind Danielle. "Do you need some help? The girls and I are good at solving mysteries."

Even if Danielle told her no, Millie had already planned to move full steam ahead with her investigation.

Danielle paused, her hand on the door handle. "Well...I like to work alone. People just seem to get in the way."

She studied Millie. "You show a lot of promise, even more than some of my colleagues." She shrugged her shoulders. "Sure. Why not?"

Chapter 15

Kay was in the cabin watching TV when they stepped back inside. She looked up as Millie closed the door. "You two get everything patched up?"

"Yep," Millie nodded. "Ariana agreed to let me handcuff myself to her."

Kay slapped the remote on her leg. "No way!"

Ariana grinned. "Are you kidding me? She'll have to wait until I'm unconscious."

Millie lifted her hands above her head. "I'm famished. Anyone care to take a run by the deli for a bite to eat?"

Ariana nodded. "Sounds good."

Kay hopped out of the chair and turned the TV off. "There's nothing like traipsing through the jungle to work up an appetite." She opened the door and waited while Ariana and Millie stepped outside. "By the way, how on earth did you make it back to the ship on time? We barely made it. They were pulling up the gangplank when we got to the dock."

Millie told Kay the story as they climbed the steps to the lido deck. Looking back now, it was funny. At the time, it had been terrifying. She wasn't sure what had been worse: seeing Ariana lying on the slab covered in red, getting lost in the jungle or watching Siren of the Seas head out to sea without her.

When they reached the deli counter, Millie let Ariana and Kay order first. Her stomach grumbled and she almost ordered two sandwiches but settled on a turkey Reuben with an extra layer of meat.

The girls wandered to a booth in the corner and Kay headed to the beverage station to grab some drinks. Millie watched her walk away. "I hope I don't accidentally call you Danielle," she fretted.

Ariana grabbed a fry and dipped it in her catsup. "Don't worry. If you do, just say that Danielle is your daughter's name and you got us mixed up."

Millie nodded. "Great idea." This girl had an answer for everything!

Ariana and Millie waited for Kay to return with their glasses of water. Millie bowed her head in silent prayer and the girls quietly waited for her to finish.

Kay grabbed the bottle of mustard and squeezed a thick line along the top of her Chicago dog. "Do they hold church services on the ship?"

Millie lifted her pickle spear and bit the end. "Yep. We have services in Sky Chapel every Sunday morning up on deck fourteen. Deck fourteen is second to the top. The chapel is at the very back."

Kay smiled. "I haven't been inside a church since I was a kid."

"The service is at 9:00 Sunday morning." Millie glanced at Ariana. "You're both welcome to come," she offered.

"I'll go," Kay answered.

"I'll think about it," Ariana said noncommittally.

The girls finished their early dinner and carried the tray of dirty dishes to the bins near the exit. They stepped outside and walked past the adults-only pool in the rear of the ship.

"That looks like fun," Kay gazed longingly at the lounging guests.

"You should put on your suit and hang out," Millie told her.

Kay glanced at Ariana. "Will you come with me?"

Ariana opened her mouth and Millie could tell the word "no" was on the tip of her tongue. Something made her change her mind. Maybe it was guilt over dragging her into the jungle or maybe she just decided it would be a nice change of pace. Either way, she agreed and the women headed down to their room to change into their bikinis while Millie headed in the opposite direction.

She decided to make her rounds and started on the lido deck. She smiled at guests enjoying what was left of the afternoon and paused for a moment to watch the children splashing around in the kiddie pool.

Andy had promised Millie he would give her some time in the children's area, but that was before Ariana Teliar aka Danielle, boarded.

Millie wandered past the kiddie splash pad and headed for the larger pool. Reggae music drifted from the upper deck and a festive tune floated in the breeze. The skies were still bright and sunny, although it was early evening.

The place was packed and now that winter up north has set in, she couldn't blame the guests for wanting to soak in all of the warmth and sunshine that they could.

Several guests stopped Millie when they recognized her from the shuttle incident. The first few times, Millie turned beet red but after a while, she just smiled and agreed it had been quite an adventure.

When she rounded the outer edge of the pool, she started down the steps when someone caught her eye. That someone was Firkin, the guy from the cave tubing excursion...the one that Christopher and Ariana had pointed out.

Millie took a step back as she slid behind a towel rack and out of sight.

Firkin, alone near the pool bar, studied the passengers. He looked like he was searching for someone. She wondered if he was looking for Ariana, or Christopher.

"Hello Millie." Millie glanced to the side. The towel attendant, Gavin, smiled at her. Gavin removed two towels that hid her from view and handed them to guests. Millie moved so that she stood behind a taller stack, still trying to keep a visual on Firkin.

Gavin gave her a curious glance.

"Just keeping an eye on one of the guests," she whispered.

He nodded. "I see."

Firkin hopped off the barstool, took one more look around the pool deck and strolled through the open doors and into the hall.

Millie darted from behind the rack in an attempt to trail him. By the time Millie got to the other side, Firkin had vanished!

Millie made a mental note to mention to Ariana...err, Danielle, that Firkin was indeed onboard Siren of the Seas.

Millie made her way through the common areas and stopped at the gift shop to make sure Cat had recovered from the docking disaster.

The store was full of shoppers and Millie glanced around. Maribelle, one of the other workers, was behind the counter. Cat was nowhere in sight.

Millie inched her way through the throng of shoppers as she made her way to the cash register.

Maribelle handed a guest his change and receipt and placed his purchases in the bag before she turned her attention to Millie.

"Where's Cat?" Millie asked.

"Down in medical. She stopped by here earlier to show me her leg. It looked like she had some sort of bite mark on her calf and it was starting to swell so I told her to have Doctor Gundervan take a look at it." Maribelle frowned. "She hasn't come back and I'm starting to worry."

Millie was already turning toward the door. "I'll go check on her."

When Millie stepped back into the corridor, she almost turned toward the kitchen to tell Annette but that would take time. Instead, she headed for the main staircase and scurried down to deck two where the medical center was located.

Millie picked up the pace as she hurried along. She hoped Cat was all right. She would feel terrible if something happened to her!

Millie could see a beam of light through the frosted glass pane. She tapped lightly on the glass and then turned the doorknob to let herself into the room.

The front reception area was empty but she could hear muffled voices from somewhere in the back.

"Hello?"

The voices stopped and a uniformed nurse appeared from the back. "Can I help you?" She glanced down at Millie's nametag.

"Yes. I heard that Cat...Catherine Wellington might be down here and I wanted to check on her." The woman nodded and then motioned her to follow her into the back.

The back room was much larger than the reception area. Hospital beds lined one wall. On the opposite side were several portable medical carts.

The room was empty except for Cat and Doctor Gundervan. Cat was sitting upright on an examining table. Doctor Gundervan had his back to Millie, his head bent close to Cat's leg.

Millie shuffled forward. She noticed that Cat's face was swollen and red.

"Millie," Cat mumbled.

Gundervan acknowledged Millie's presence with a quick glance.

"Maribelle told me you had some sort of bite on your leg," Millie said.

Cat nodded.

Gundervan spoke. "It appears she is having a toxic reaction to a bite she got while she was traipsing through the jungle." He gave Millie a disapproving frown. "The area around the bite continues to swell and I may have to give her an anti-venom shot."

Cat shuddered. "I hate needles."

Gundervan turned concerned eyes to Cat. "I promise I will make it as painless as possible." He touched her arm.

Millie reached over and grabbed Cat's hand. "I'll stay here with you," she offered.

Gundervan waited while the nurse made her way over to one of the cabinets. She reached inside and pulled out a vial. After the nurse prepared the needle, she handed the needle to Doctor Gundervan.

Cat's eyes were as round as saucers as she stared at the needle in his hand. "Are you sure we can't wait this out?"

Gundervan set the needle on the tray nearby. He shoved his hands into the pockets of his medical jacket. "I'll make you a deal. If you aren't running a fever, we wait. If you are running a fever, you take the shot."

Cat nodded. That sounded fair. "Okay."

The nurse pulled a thermometer from the drawer, rolled it across Cat's forehead and then studied the screen. "An even 101."

"Cat, you have a fever," Gundervan explained. "You are having a toxic reaction and need the anti-venom shot."

He lifted the huge needle from the tray. It was Millie's turn for her eyes to widen.

Cat started to shake her head.

Gundervan was firm. "Tell you what," he bargained, "You be a good girl and let me give you this shot and I'll give you a lollipop," he teased.

Cat's grin was lopsided; the muscles in her face had grown numb.

Gundervan was right! Cat needed that shot ASAP!

Millie leaned in to try to distract Cat. "Cat, if you take that shot, I promise to never drag you into the jungle again."

Cat turned her attention to Millie and at that precise moment, Gundervan inserted the needle into her upper thigh.

Cat jerked upright. "Ouch!" she yelped.

Gundervan pulled the needle out and patted her leg. "You did it, Cat."

He went on. "I would like to keep an eye on you for a few hours. Just relax now and we'll get you settled into one of these nice cozy beds. Take your pick."

Cat eyed the row of empty beds. "Whichever one is furthest away from the needles."

Gundervan grinned as he put his arm around Cat to help her down from the examining table. Millie took a step back to get out of the way.

There was a spark between Gundervan and Cat. Maybe it was the way that he looked at her...or maybe it was the way she looked up at him with adoring eyes...although that could be caused by the shot or venom from the bite.

Millie lowered her gaze to Gundervan's right hand. He was wearing a band but someone had once told her that he wasn't married.

Gundervan and the nurse settled Cat into one of the beds and tucked the covers around her. "I'll be back soon to check on you," he promised before he turned and made his way to the front room.

The nurse grabbed the used medical tools and headed for the sanitizing area on the other side of the room.

Millie pulled a chair close to Cat's bed.

"I feel fine," Cat insisted.

"You look like a watermelon head," Millie said.

"Thanks! Some friend you are."

Millie cupped her hands together and whispered in Cat's ear. "He likes you."

"Who?"

"Doctor Gundervan."

Cat frowned. "So? He probably likes a lot of people."

"No," Millie insisted, "he *likes* you. You know…" She lowered her eyelids seductively.

Cat's face turned a deeper shade of red. "He does not!"

Millie lifted her shoulders. "Hm."

Cat glanced over Millie's shoulder at Gundervan. "But I'm too old for him."

Millie waved an arm. "Shoot! You're a hottie, girl. Why this could be one of those May-December relationships blossoming!"

Cat slapped her arm. "Stop that!"

"Cat the Cougar," Millie teased.

The nurse headed their way and Millie quieted down. She took Cat's temperature again and then wrapped a blood pressure cuff around her arm. "Already an improvement," she said after she finished.

Convinced that Cat was in capable hands, Millie stood. "I better get back to Ariana."

Cat frowned. "Did she make it back on board?"

Millie nodded. So much had happened since the girls' adventurous embarkation; she hadn't had a chance to tell them that Ariana was an imposter. "Boy, have I got a tale for you, but I'll wait 'til you're back on your feet."

Millie headed for the door. She turned around, motioned to the back of Gundervan's head and winked.

Cat made a slashing motion across her neck. "Cut it out!" she mouthed.

Millie grinned and began to whistle as she exited the medical center. Yep, Cat was on the path to a little shipboard romance!

Chapter 16

Millie found Ariana lounging in a chair next to the adults-only pool…alone. She settled into the chair next to her. "What happened to your sidekick?"

Ariana opened one eye and glanced at Millie. "Kay said it was too hot so she went down to the cabin."

"Where did you run off to?" Ariana asked.

Millie shifted in the chair. "Just making my rounds." She remembered Firkin. "Say, I saw that guy, Firkin. He was over at the bar area next to the pool on the other side of the ship."

Ariana lifted her head and stared at Millie. "You're kidding."

Millie shook her head. "Nope. I tried to sneak up on him but by the time I got over there, he had disappeared."

Ariana lowered her head and tapped her fingernail on the armrest. "Christopher told me Firkin didn't get on the ship."

"Maybe he just didn't see him."

"I'll give him the benefit of the doubt. If you see Chris, don't mention that you saw Firkin. Let's wait and see if he tells us," Ariana told her.

"Okay," Millie agreed. "Have you been working on a plan to flush out the killer?"

Ariana ran her fingers through her long blonde hair. "Yeah. This one is kind of tricky, being confined to a cruise ship and all."

Millie thought back to the handful of cases she'd worked on so far. "You're telling me."

She needed to have a meeting with Cat and Annette so they could put their heads together. "Maybe later, after tonight's headliner show, we can get together with the other girls and try to come up with a plan."

Ariana slipped her sunglasses on and leaned her head back in the chair. "We just need to make sure no one sees us."

"They won't," Millie reassured her. "We can meet in the galley after hours. Why don't we plan on 11:00 p.m.? If we get separated, meet me in front of Formals, the tuxedo shop."

"You got it." Ariana gave her the thumbs up and Millie stood. Although it was late in the day, it was still hot outside. Of course, Millie was in full uniform and Ariana was in a bikini. Millie had to admit, the girl was in great shape. Being an undercover agent, she supposed one would have to be...

Millie's next stop was the kitchen to set up a rendezvous with Annette. She hoped that Cat would be back on her feet by then.

On her way, she made a quick stop by the gift shop to let Maribelle know that Cat would be all right, but that she would have to cover for her for a while longer.

Maribelle smoothed a wayward strand of hair from her eyes. "As long as Cat is going to be okay, I can cover the rest of the shift."

Millie headed back out and made her way to the side door that led into the kitchen. Annette was nowhere in sight. Amit, Annette's right hand man, was standing next to a large commercial grade mixer. Flour was flying everywhere. Millie smiled. If Annette could see the mess Amit was making, she would have a fit!

Millie wound her way past several counters and approached Amit. "Whatcha making?"

Amit shut the mixer off. "I make a special surprise for Miss Annette. It is her birthday tomorrow."

Millie frowned. "I didn't know that." Annette probably didn't want her to know that, either. Millie couldn't even buy her friend a gift! Or could she? She remembered Andy had mentioned meeting with his friend, the one that sold Taser guns, the last time they'd been in Miami.

"Thanks, Amit." She turned to go. "By the way, where is Annette?"

"Down in the crew mess. There was a problem with one of the rice dishes." He shrugged. "I am sure she will sort it out."

Millie was sure she would, too! She headed down to crew mess and found Annette behind the hot line, scolding one of the crew.

Annette tapped the top of a large metal pot with the tip of a wooden spoon. "...which will turn the rice into mush. You must not put too much water in it when you cook it." She rolled her eyes. "If you ever want to move up the ranks and work in my kitchen, you need to pay attention to details."

Judging by the look on the poor man's face, she wasn't sure that he *would* want to work with Annette in her kitchen. Sometimes Annette came across as a little...overbearing. Underneath that gruff exterior, though, was a heart of gold.

Millie approached the counter. "Ahem!"

Annette jerked her head. The stern expression disappeared. "Hi Millie."

"You got a minute?"

The relief on the poor crew's face was palpable and Millie winked at him.

Annette followed Millie to a table for two and they settled in. "Cat is in medical."

"Why?"

"Something bit her in the jungle and she had an allergic reaction," Millie explained. "She's going to be okay."

Millie leaned in. "I think there's a little spark between Cat and Doctor Gundervan."

Annette raised a brow. "Isn't he..."

"Younger?" Millie prompted. "Yeah, but does that matter?"

"True."

"Cat the Cougar," Millie said.

She changed the subject. "That's not why I'm here. I was wondering if we could get together around 11:00 this evening in the kitchen. I have new information on the case."

"Sure," Annette said. "The kitchen should be empty by then. Speaking of that, I should get back there. Hard telling what kind of mess Amit has gotten into."

Millie nodded innocently. If she only knew…which reminded her. "You never told me your birthday was tomorrow!"

Annette slid out of the chair and stood. "Let me guess. Big mouth Amit told you."

"It's a good thing he did. I would've been mad if he hadn't!"

Annette shrugged and started for the door. "Another birthday. Big deal."

"It is a big deal," Millie argued.

The women wandered down the I-95 corridor as they made their way to the guest area. When they got to the third deck, Millie stopped. "I need to check in with Andy. See you at eleven."

Annette nodded and started up the next level. "Okie doke."

Millie stepped inside the dark theater. Her eyes scanned the upper level and she paused when she caught sight of the door that led to Ariana's suite.

She made her way down the center aisle and then up the steps that skirted the side of the stage. The back of the stage was quiet and empty, except for a dim light beaming out from Andy's small office.

She found Andy sitting at the table, his head bent down as he studied his notebook.

"Ahem."

Andy lifted his head and removed his reading glasses. "Hello Millie. I saw you on the lido deck earlier, by the pool."

Millie nodded. "I made my rounds and then stopped to check on Ariana."

"How is Ariana?"

Millie slid into the seat next to him. "I think we're safe on that front. Things are not as they seem, though."

Andy clasped his hands together. Millie had his undivided attention. "What do you mean?"

"That Ariana is not who you think she is and the list of suspects in Miguel's murder is growing." She had a thought. "Speaking of that, how is Dave Patterson doing on his end of the investigation?"

"He has several suspects but no arrests...yet."

"Someone close to Ariana?" Millie prompted.

"You'll have to ask Patterson yourself. He's about as forthright with information as you."

Andy stuck the tip of his glasses in his mouth and studied Millie. "One more day and then you're off the hook. You think you can keep Ariana alive and out of trouble for one more day?"

"Piece of cake," Millie said. "Not to change the subject, but Annette's birthday is tomorrow and I don't have a gift."

She went on. "When you met with your friend at that gun shop in Miami last week, you didn't happen to have picked up a few Tasers."

"I did," he said. "You want to give one to Annette for her birthday?"

Millie nodded. Annette had mentioned during Andy's recent Taser demonstration that she wanted to buy one.

"I bought several but some of those are spoken for. I think I might have one or two extra."

"I'll bring it back here before the evening performance," he promised.

"Great! Just let me know how much I owe you," she added gratefully.

Andy shook his head. "No charge. Just be sure to pick up a card and put both of our names on it."

Millie impulsively reached over and hugged Andy's neck. Sudden tears burned the back of her eyes. "You're the best and I miss you."

She released her grip and hurried out of the room lest she burst into tears and embarrass herself.

Chapter 17

Millie climbed the stairs that ran along the side of the theater as she made her way over to Ariana's suite. She tapped on the door and Kay opened it. She stood off to the side to let Millie enter. "She's in the shower."

Kay flopped down on the sofa and picked up the remote. "Are you going to watch the show tonight?"

Millie settled into the chair near the desk. "Yep. Tonight is the production of Grease. It's a good one. You don't want to miss it."

Kay flipped through the TV channels. "Yeah. Maybe," she said noncommittally. "I'm on the fence about it. Ariana doesn't have another performance until tomorrow night and I was thinking of hanging out in the piano bar instead."

"You can do both," Millie pointed out.

"True," Kay agreed. "I dunno."

Ariana emerged from the bathroom and once again, Millie was struck by how young she looked without the thick layer of makeup she normally wore. "You look much better without all that makeup."

Ariana finished towel drying her hair and picked up the hairbrush lying on the counter. "Do you think so? I've worn makeup for so long, I feel naked without it."

Millie glanced down at Ariana's wrist and the fake scar. Danielle was good. Millie had to give her that. She rarely slipped up and if she did, Millie wasn't able to catch it. "The show is in an hour. Are you going to go?"

Ariana started to shake her head and then changed her mind. "Sure." She turned to Kay. "Will you go with us?"

Kay shrugged her shoulders. "Yeah. I guess I'll go." She flipped the TV off and stood, stretching her arms above her head. "First I have to get ready."

Kay crossed the room and wandered into her own small cabin, closing the door behind her.

Ariana paused, the hairbrush in midair. "She's acting weird today. I think she's suspicious."

"Of what?" Millie asked.

"That you and I are no longer at odds. Maybe we need to fake a fight," Ariana added.

Ariana didn't wait for Millie to reply before she shoved Millie's arm. She raised her voice. "I'm getting sick and tired of you following me around like a lost puppy. Maybe I don't want to go to the show," she shrieked shrilly.

Millie played along. She stuck her hand on her hip. The door to the cabin next door opened a crack. "Listen, I've got a little over 24 hours to put up with your antics and I've had it about up to here." She raised her hand above her head. "You will stay with me if I have to superglue our hips together!"

Ariana tossed her airbrush on the counter and flounced into the bathroom, slamming the door behind her.

"Good. Stay there. At least I know where you're at," Millie muttered.

Kay opened the door wider. "I hope they're giving you double pay for having to deal with that one."

She didn't wait for a reply as she closed the door and left Millie in the suite all alone. Millie waited for Ariana to come out of the bathroom for several long moments and then gave up. She opened the door to the balcony and stepped outside.

The sun had set and the stars were shining brightly in the clear night sky. Millie wished she had a balcony in her cabin.

Ariana joined her several minutes later. "She bought it hook, line and sinker."

Millie nodded. "We're on for the 11:00 meeting in the kitchen. What will we do if Kay insists on tagging along?"

Ariana ran her fingers through her hair. "We'll find a way to lose her, just like I did you."

True. Ariana had a knack for losing people. Millie guessed that it went along with the territory.

By the time the girls wandered out into the theater, the first act was over and the entertainment staff had just started the second act. The place was packed and they couldn't find three empty seats so they stood near the back.

Millie watched her friends with pride. She studied the faces of the guests in the theater. They all seemed to enjoy the show.

Millie counted her blessings and appreciated all that she had. So what if Ariana had been an inconvenience...a big inconvenience? It had also been an adventure and somewhat fun, except for the part where she had to board the ship from the shuttle boat...

The show was mesmerizing and it moved at a fast pace, but the stress from the day had finally caught up with Millie and she began to feel drowsy. She leaned her arm on the railing in front of her and closed her eyes.

"Psst!" Ariana nudged Millie's arm. "Hey! Sleeping Beauty."

Millie's eyes flew open. Had she actually dozed off standing up?

"The show is over," Ariana said.

She was right. The show had ended and the room brightened. Kay was nowhere in sight. "What happened to Kay?"

Ariana shrugged. "She got bored and took off. All the better for us."

Millie had to agree. They had another hour and a half before they were to meet Annette and

Cat in the kitchen. "I think she mentioned she wanted to go to the piano bar so as long as we stay away from there, we should be safe."

The girls wandered out of the theater. The odds of them running into Pierre, Christopher, Firkin or Kay were high. They needed a place to hide out for a while and Millie had the perfect spot in mind!

***

Millie opened the door to Sky Chapel and waited for Ariana to follow her inside. The only light they could see came from behind a small cross that hung on the wall in the front.

Ariana glanced around. "So this is what the inside of a church looks like."

"Chapel," Millie corrected.

"Chapel."

Ariana shivered. "It's cool and sorta creepy."

Millie didn't think it was creepy. She thought it was peaceful and she felt God's presence. In fact, she had visited the place many times since she'd started working on Siren of the Seas. It was her sanctuary when she felt stressed out and needed a few quiet moments alone with God.

The girls slid onto a nearby bench and Millie closed her eyes to pray. She asked the Lord to protect them and to help them solve the mystery of who was trying to kill Ariana...Danielle.

When she opened her eyes, she gave Ariana a sideways glance. The young woman's eyes had glazed over and a lone tear slid down her cheek.

Millie looked straight ahead and pretended not to notice. Ariana's shoulders began to tremble slightly. Millie grabbed the young woman's hand and squeezed lightly.

"I haven't been in church for years," she whispered. "Do you think God remembers me?"

Millie's eyes began to burn and her heart lurched at the thought that this woman thought that God had forgotten about her. "God never forgets His children. You may have stepped away from Him, but He never stepped away from you."

"He is tugging at your heart, right now," Millie added.

Ariana popped off the bench and shuffled to the front of the sanctuary where she knelt on the floor in front of the cross.

Ariana clasped her hands together and bowed her head.

Millie closed her eyes and began to pray for Ariana. Although Millie didn't know what to pray, God did.

The young woman stayed at the altar for a long time and finally...slowly rose to her feet. She returned to where Millie was still waiting as she dabbed at her eyes with the back of her hand.

"Is the offer still open to come to church with you?"

Millie grinned and nodded as Ariana settled beside her, once again. "You betcha!"

She lifted her wrist and stared at her watch. The hour was late and it was almost time to meet Annette and Cat in the kitchen. Millie slowly rose to her feet. "C'mon. It's time to head to the kitchen and put a plan in place."

Ariana followed Millie out of the quiet sanctuary, glancing back one last time before they headed out onto the lido deck.

Chapter 18

Annette and Cat were already in the kitchen when Millie and Ariana wandered in.

Millie walked over to Cat and put an arm around her shoulder. "Are you feeling better? How is the bite?"

Cat glanced down at her leg. "Much better."

"Good. Now for a bigger question...How is Doctor Gundervan?"

Cat turned a hint of pink. She waved her hand. "He's fine."

"Do you have a date yet?" Millie probed.

Cat groaned. "Will you stop with the romance stuff?"

Millie could see Cat wasn't in the mood. She turned her attention to the baking supplies that covered the large, stainless steel counter. "What are we making this time?" Millie asked.

"Since Thanksgiving is right around the corner, it's time to add my pumpkin pecan cobbler to the dessert menu."

Millie's mouth watered. It sounded delicious, and if Annette was going to make it, Millie knew it had to be good.

The girls began to work; each assigned a different task, except for Ariana, who stood off to the side to watch. "You don't want me to help. I can burn water," she joked.

Annette began to mix the dry ingredients in a large bowl while Millie dumped everything else into another bowl.

Annette gave Cat the task of mixing the topping and when Millie saw the pecans, she decided she would have to try the recipe when she got home.

Annette turned to Ariana. "You're in a jam and we're going to help you out, but to do that, we need the whole story. Start at the beginning."

Ariana gave Millie a quick glance and Millie nodded her head. "Go ahead. Tell them everything. You can trust them."

Ariana sucked in a breath and began her tale. "First of all, my name isn't Ariana Teliar. It's Danielle Kneldon. I'm not the daughter of a rich investor. I'm a cop-for-hire. I hold a Master Black Belt and also make money as a trainer when I'm not working undercover."

She lunged forward and lifted her hands in a pose.

Annette dropped the fork she'd been using to sift the flour and salt. "Well, I'll be darned. I have a brown belt. I always wanted to make it to the black belt." She lunged forward as she mimicked Ariana's pose.

Millie raised a brow. She had long suspected there was more to Annette than met the eye. She remembered the time they were in Jamaica and Annette took down a would-be thief that had tried to rob them.

She hoped that someday Annette would come clean and tell the girls why she always seemed to have tracking devices, listening devices and all the other James Bond-type equipment on hand.

Ariana continued to tell them that Jacob Gatwick had hired her after someone had murdered his daughter's personal assistant, mistaking the poor woman for Ariana.

Danielle had stepped in, pretending to be the daughter while the real Ariana jetted off to a remote location. A location that Danielle herself did not even know.

"At the time of the assistant's death, Gatwick had been close to uncovering treasures from an ancient Mayan civilization, rumored to have buried tons of gold and precious jewels in one of the Mayan ruins yet to be excavated."

She went on. "He knew he was being watched so he formulated a plan to not only flush out Ariana's would-be killer, but also have me bring back solid evidence of the lost civilization's existence."

"Which was what you were doing when you disappeared in Costa Maya during the cave tubing," Millie interjected.

"Right," Danielle agreed. "Because Gatwick didn't completely trust me, he sent Christopher Johnson along."

"How did you know where to look?" Cat asked.

"Jacob Gatwick gave me a photocopy of a map he believed led to the lost city."

The pieces were all starting to fall into place for Millie. "So that's what was in the fanny pack that you were so determined to keep with you."

"Nope." Danielle shook her head. "The bag was just a decoy to throw everyone off."

This was right out of a 007 movie! Millie rubbed her hands together. "Any chance we can take a look at the map?" She'd never seen a treasure map, or in this case, an archaeological map.

Three sets of expectant eyes turned to Danielle. She sucked in a deep breath. "Okay."

Millie thought she would reach into the fanny pack, still attached to her hip.

Instead, she lifted her blouse, reached inside her bra and pulled out a small folded piece of paper.

The girls dropped what they were doing and surrounded Danielle. Millie fumbled for her reading glasses and then peered at the sheet of paper that Danielle had unfolded.

Millie expected to see some sort of cool map. The one that Danielle set on the counter didn't look like much. There were sketches of mountains, a few x's and some weird symbols that she didn't understand.

Annette wrinkled her nose. "This map led you to a lost civilization?"

Danielle pointed at one of the symbols with her index finger. "That's it."

Millie leaned in. On closer inspection, she could see a small winding river, which could easily be mistaken for a snake. She correctly guessed it to be the river where they had gone tubing.

"You'd have to know what you were looking for," she explained. Danielle carefully folded the map and shoved it back inside her bra.

"I have a question," Cat said. "What in the world were you doing, lying on top of that slab of cement in the middle of the jungle?"

Danielle snorted. "I was trying to flush out the killer." She shrugged. "I very well might have if you guys hadn't 'rescued' me!"

"You could've been killed," Annette pointed out.

"True," Danielle admitted. "But that wasn't my plan."

Annette returned to mixing as she grabbed the smaller bowl of ingredients Millie had blended. She dumped them into the larger bowl and started to stir. "Who is on the suspect list?"

Danielle lifted her index finger. "One. Kay, my assistant. Two. Pierre my PR guy. Three. Firkin."

She shrugged. "I think that's it."

"What about Christopher?" Millie asked.

Danielle shook her head. "I think he's clean. I had him checked out after Gatwick hired him."

"We only have one more day to crack this case," Cat pointed out.

Annette dumped the blended ingredients in a large square baking dish and popped it in the preheated oven. "Do you think whoever it is still plans to kill you?"

Danielle nodded. "I do, but I'm quite certain that before they do that, they want to make sure they have the map." She patted her blouse. "Over my dead body."

"We hope not," Millie said. "So we need a plan to flush the person or persons out."

Millie grabbed a stack of dirty dishes and headed to the sink. "Tomorrow night is your final performance."

Annette slapped her open palm on the counter. "I have it! I have an idea!"

Annette outlined the plan. It seemed like a good one based on the short amount of time they had left.

Ariana turned to Annette. "Are you sure you want to do this?"

Annette snapped her fingers. "Piece of cake."

The girls finalized the details and agreed to use Cat as the middleman if they needed to relay information. Since she worked in the gift shop, it would not look suspicious if the girls just happened to stop by there.

***

Millie slept fitfully on the cot that night. She wasn't sure if it was because it was so darned uncomfortable or if it was from worrying about Ariana's stalker.

She thought about Kay in the cabin next door. What if it was Kay and she snuck out of her cabin and murdered Ariana...or both of them in their sleep?

She must have finally dozed off because next thing she knew, bright light was peeking through the edge of the curtain and Ariana was gone. Once again, she had vanished.

Kay emerged from her cabin bleary-eyed. She looked around the room. "Ariana is gone!"

Kay plopped down on the edge of Ariana's unmade bed. "Figures."

Millie had given up on keeping tabs on Ariana. Instead, she decided that since Ariana was gone, she would get ready and then run up to Captain Armati's apartment to see if she could take Scout out, at least for a little while. She missed him like crazy.

When Millie reached the bridge, she let herself in. Captain Armati was off in the corner, talking on the phone. He smiled when he saw Millie.

A warm heat rushed over Millie's body as she remembered their kiss.

She pointed toward his apartment and he nodded as he continued to talk, his eyes following her.

Millie punched in the key code and opened the door. Scout wasn't waiting at the door, which was unusual. Millie called his name as she wandered into the living room.

Her eyes searched the room and she finally found him, buried in his box of stuffed animals. He opened his eyes and glanced at Millie.

Millie rushed over to his toy box. Her first thought was that he was sick. She dropped to her knees and reached out to pet him.

"Hey Scout. Are you okay?" He licked the tip of her finger and then closed his eyes.

"He has been like that all morning." The captain had followed her into the apartment.

Millie looked up. "Do you think he's mad at me?"

Captain smiled and shook his head. "No. He's just lonely and bored. I think with a little persuasion he'll come around."

Millie got to her feet and headed for the slider. "You want to go outside?"

Scout's ears perked up. He slowly ambled out of the toy box and followed her onto the balcony.

The captain followed them out. They watched as Scout slowly trotted to his green space and watered the fake grass.

When he finished, he made his way over to Millie and pawed at her leg. Millie picked him up and held him close. "Would you like to go with me today?"

Scout began to wiggle in her arms. "Woof."

It was as if he understood what she was saying and he probably did. She set him on the deck. "Let's go, Scout! Let's go make our rounds."

Scout raced off into the living room and toward the apartment door.

Millie grinned. "I think you're right." She gazed back at Captain Armati. "Is it okay if he goes with me today?"

"Yes! Please take him!" the captain replied. "I can't stand to see that sad little face staring at me any longer."

They followed Scout to the hall, where he had planted himself in front of the door.

Millie leaned down and reached for his carrier. "Okay. Okay. Let me get your bag."

Millie adjusted the bag on her shoulder while Captain Armati opened the door. "We'll be back before dinner," she promised.

The captain nodded. "Perhaps we can have dinner one evening next week before I leave."

Millie blushed. "I would like that."

Millie stepped into the bridge and watched as Scout darted back and forth across the floor. He made a pass by and Millie stopped him as she hooked his leash to his collar. "Can't have you running off in all the excitement to be free."

The captain walked them to the exit door and waited while they stepped into the hall. "Stay out of trouble."

Millie grinned. "We'll try."

She was glad for the distraction that Scout gave and enjoyed watching him as he visited with several of the ship's passengers. She made a point to stop by Scout's oasis so he could take a dip in his pool.

After his swim, they headed to the lido for a bite to eat. Millie picked up a slice of roasted turkey, Scout's favorite. She watched as he devoured his treat.

Millie had made a brief stop by Andy's office to beg him to let her at least do some of her normal duties. He relented and even seemed relieved.

Scout and Millie hosted a round of trivia near the casino bar. They helped with bingo in the theater and then Scout and she made their way to guest services to find out if there were any passenger complaints about the entertainment.

Nikki, who was one of Sarah's friends, was working behind the counter. She looked up as Scout and Millie approached.

Nikki reached out to pet Scout. "Oh! Hey fella. Where have you two been?"

Millie groaned. "Babysitting but it's almost over." She set Scout on the floor and he ran under the door to the back to say "hello" to the staff working behind the counter.

Millie watched him disappear. "Have there been any passenger complaints on entertainment?"

Nikki held up a finger. "Let me check."

She wandered to the side and consulted the others. She returned and shook her head. "Nope. You're good to go."

Millie was relieved. She knew that her having to watch Ariana had taken its toll on Andy and that he had had to wear two hats: his and hers!

Scout made his way back to her side and Millie picked him up and tucked him in the crook of her arm. She lifted Scout's paw and they waved good-bye as they headed to security.

Millie had one more stop to make...Dave Patterson's office.

Chapter 19

Millie's heart sank when she noticed that Patterson's office was dark and the door closed. "That was a waste of time," Millie muttered.

The two of them turned to go and they started back down the long hall. They made it as far as the door leading into the passenger area. Millie opened the door. Patterson was on the other side.

"Just the person I was looking for," Millie said. "You got a minute?"

Patterson nodded. "Sure. Let's go to my office."

Millie walked alongside Patterson as they made their way back down the corridor. "Let me guess. This has something to do with Ariana Teliar and Miguel."

"Yep."

Scout began to wiggle and Millie set him on the gleaming concrete floor where he darted off down the hall.

Patterson unlocked his office door and flipped on the light before he stepped aside to let Millie and Scout in.

Patterson stepped around the side of his desk and settled into his chair. Scout began to explore Patterson's office, a place he had never visited before.

Millie kept one eye on Scout and the other on Patterson. "Do you have any suspects in Miguel's murder?"

Patterson picked up the pen on his desk and pressed the button on the end. "Yes, and all of them involve Ariana Teliar."

Millie nodded. That made sense since they had found Miguel's body on Ariana's balcony.

Patterson set the pen down. "You're close to Ariana. Who do you think it is?"

"Kay, the assistant, Pierre, the PR person or another man that goes by the name Firkin."

"What about Christopher Johnson? I hear he spends a lot of time with Ariana."

Millie shrugged. "Could be, but I'm not leaning in that direction."

Millie leaned forward in her chair. "I have a question."

Patterson lifted a brow.

"What was Miguel's assignment the day he was murdered?"

Patterson leaned back in his chair and crossed his arms. "Security. Passport inspection."

Millie continued. "Could it be that Miguel found something...maybe something on a passenger's passport that looked out of place? When he questioned the person, they killed him to keep him quiet?"

Patterson slowly nodded. "Yes. In fact, I have personnel checking each and every passport on board, but there are almost 3,000 passengers on this cruise and it takes time."

"Unless you can link them to Ariana," she said.

"Unless I can link them to Ariana," he agreed. "Would someone be that careless?"

Millie paused, the wheels spinning in her head. "What if...Miguel was on his way to confront the suspect, who happened to be near Ariana's suite? They got into an argument. Miguel was murdered and in a panic, the killer left his body on the balcony?"

"The only people who had access to Ariana's suite would be staff with a master key, or someone who was staying in the suite and had their own key card."

Millie remembered the half door she had discovered on the balcony. She wondered where that door led. She made a mental note to check it out as soon as she left Patterson's office.

Millie spent the rest of the afternoon mulling over the information. They were so close, yet so far!

When she reached Ariana's suite, it was empty. Kay was gone. Ariana was gone. Millie let herself in and made a beeline for the balcony. She left Scout inside the cabin, afraid that he would get too close to the large gap in the railing and tumble overboard.

She closed the balcony door behind her and turned to study the half door. She knelt down and pushed on the door, which was locked.

She leaned forward and peered around the corner. On the other side was a small walkway, which led to another half door.

If only she could figure out where it went!

"What are you doing?"

Millie nearly jumped out of her skin. Her hand flew to her chest. It was Ariana. "You scared the crap out of me!"

"Sorry." Ariana repeated herself. "What are you doing?"

"Trying to figure out what's beyond that half door."

"Let's open it up and find out. Be right back." Ariana disappeared inside the room. She returned moments later with a metal tool that looked like something a dentist would use.

Millie stepped to the side while Ariana knelt down and inserted the blunt edge of the tool into the key hole. She twisted it a couple times and then "click," the door swung open. "Piece of cake."

Ariana ducked down and crawled through the half door. Millie dropped down on all fours and followed her. There was nothing on the other side except for a solid wall of metal bulkhead.

Ariana opened the second door and the girls, once again, crawled through the half door. When they got to the third catwalk, there was another door, but this one was on the side of the ship and the door was almost full size.

Ariana studied it. She narrowed her eyes. "This might be trickier." It took several tries but Ariana was persistent and finally, the lock popped.

She grabbed the metal door pull and gave it a swift tug. The door creaked open and the girls stepped inside...and into the lobby right outside the theater.

Millie had never noticed the door before. Of course, the ship was full of side doors and secret hallways that passengers - and crew - never noticed.

She stuck a hand on her hip. "Well, I'll be darned. I had no idea."

The girls retraced their steps, careful to shut and lock the doors as they retraced their steps.

Ariana slipped the small tool in her blouse.

Millie gave her a funny look.

Ariana shrugged. "It's the only place I can keep track of stuff."

The girls made it back to the balcony just moments before Kay returned!

Millie shuffled inside, grabbed Scout's leash and the two of them headed for the door. "We need to check in with Andy," she explained.

They headed down the center steps and Scout picked up the pace when he realized where they were going.

When they got close to the stage, Scout darted up the side steps.

The entertainment staff was practicing for the evening performance and Scout headed right into the thick of the action. He pranced in circles, excited to see his friends.

Millie smiled down at him. She knew she would miss Scout when the captain was on leave. She vowed to spend as much time as possible with both of them before they left.

The day flew by and finally it was time to take Scout home. Millie had tuckered him out and his trot had turned to a slow stroll. Millie picked him up and he leaned his head against her shoulder.

The bridge was quiet. Captain Vitale was the only one at the helm.

Captain Armati was nowhere in sight. Millie let Scout inside and then headed back out.

The countdown had begun and Millie returned to Ariana's suite to put the plan to flush out Miguel's killer into motion!

Ariana had already gone into actor mode when Millie let herself in the room. "Millie, you'll watch my performance tonight, won't you?"

Millie nodded. "Yes, of course. I think we should all go." Her eyes slid to Kay, who was nearby watching TV.

"Even Pierre," Ariana insisted.

Kay crossed her arms. "Even Pierre."

"Good," Ariana puckered her lips.

The stage had been set...the wheels in motion. Now all they had to do was wait...

***

Annette studied the ladder that hung from the side of the stage and connected with the catwalk. The catwalk was a long, narrow strip of metal, with just enough room for one person to crawl across.

Bundles of thick electrical wires hung low, leaving little room for a person to squeeze through.

Annette glanced to the left. The makeup and dressing room were buzzing with excited voices as the troupe prepared for the evening's performance.

She glanced to the right. Andy's office was dark and she was the only one backstage.

Soft strains of music floated up from the orchestra pit – her cue that the show was about to begin.

Annette scrambled up the ladder and crawled onto the catwalk. She slithered along the metal plank until she had a clear view of the stage below…and Ariana's fanny pack strategically dropped near the back wall.

She pulled her cellphone from her back pocket and placed it on the grate next to her.

Now all she had to do was to wait for Millie to do her part...to let the killer know the fanny pack was ripe for the picking!

***

Millie's heart pounded as the curtains went up and Ariana took the stage. Millie had spent a token amount of time behind the stage before returning to her seat, front and center. Kay and Pierre sat to Millie's right. The only suspect left was Firkin and she hadn't been able to track him down.

Ariana had a beautiful, lyrical voice and if not for the overwhelming feeling of impending doom, Millie would have enjoyed the performance.

Ariana sang her heart out, as if she had not a care in the world.

The first part of the performance finished with nary a hitch and there was a brief intermission when the lights went up.

"I wonder how Ariana's doing," Millie mused.

"She's doing great," Kay said.

"No. I mean, without her fanny pack. She couldn't fit it under her costume and Andy made her take it off."

She pointed off to the left corner. "It's off in that far corner, sitting there on the floor." Millie shrugged. "I guess she thought one of the other entertainers might steal it."

Pierre nodded. "She keeps that thing on night and day. It's like her security blanket."

The trio chatted for several more moments. The lights began to dim. Pierre abruptly stood. "I better use the bathroom. Too much coffee," he joked.

The girls watched him leave and Ariana began part two of her performance.

Pierre returned several minutes later and settled back into his seat.

Millie stared at him expectantly. He rubbed his stomach. "Gotta watch out for that midnight buffet."

Kay rolled her eyes. "Spare us the details."

Halfway through the second half, Kay excused herself to use the restroom.

She returned just as Ariana finished her performance. The rest of the dancers took the stage for the grand finale and when it ended, the lights went up.

The three of them waited until the crowd thinned before they climbed out of their chairs and headed out of the theater.

Millie stared at the back of the heads of the suspects. She couldn't wait to track down Annette and find out what happened backstage and if Pierre or Kay had made a move for the pack.

Chapter 20

There was only one way off the catwalk. Annette shimmied backwards until she reached the ladder on the wall. It was pitch black and she couldn't see behind her.

She stuck her foot out and ran it along the wall as she searched for the rung. When her foot hit hard surface, she slithered back until her other foot reached the rung. With both feet firmly in place, she swiveled around and began the slow descent down.

"What in the world?" a deep voice echoed from below. It was Andy.

Annette hopped off the bottom step and swiped her hand across the front of her pants. "Always wondered what was up there."

"I don't buy that for one minute, Annette Delacroix," Andy bellowed. "You are up to something!"

Millie heard Andy before she saw him. "We were trying to flush out Miguel's killer."

Andy slapped a hand to his forehead. "You two are giving me gray hair!"

"Too late," Millie teased.

Ariana emerged from the dressing room. Cat was with her. "Well?"

Andy had no idea what they were talking about but decided to chime in. "Well?"

Annette's shoulders slumped. "Nothing. Nada. Zip. No one showed up." She shook her head. "I don't understand!"

Millie couldn't either. She was certain that whoever it was, would show up for the fanny pack! Unless it was Firkin…

The group wandered out of the theater area and into the main lobby. Annette's radio buzzed. "Annette, are you there?" It was Amit.

Annette pulled her radio and lifted it to her lips. "Go ahead."

"We need you in the kitchen. We have a small emergency," he explained.

Annette groaned. "This late at night? He has got to be kidding!"

She headed for the kitchen with Cat, Andy, Ariana and Millie hot on her heels. Millie grabbed Andy's arm. "You got it?"

He nodded and patted the pocket of his jacket.

Annette made it to the side kitchen door in record time and the rest had to hurry to keep up with her.

The round porthole window leading into the kitchen was dark. "What in the world? Why are all the lights off?"

Annette shoved the door open and barreled inside.

"Surprise!" The lights came on and illuminated the entire kitchen staff who had crowded around the long counter.

Amit, who was front and center, carefully walked down the aisle, birthday cake in hand. "Happy birthday to you…"

The employees began to sing. Annette teared up. "How? Why?"

"Because we love you," Millie hugged her friend.

Annette blew out the candles and everyone cheered. Amit sliced the carrot cake, Annette's favorite, and passed plates of cake around the room. Millie was impressed. Amit had baked Annette the biggest two-layer birthday cake she had ever seen!

The cake was delicious and Millie complimented him on not only hiding the cake from Annette, but also remembering her birthday.

Amit shoved his hands in his pockets and stared at the floor. When he looked up, his expression was somber. "No one would give me a chance in the kitchen...no one but Miss Annette."

The room grew silent as Amit continued to tell his story. "If not for her, I would be in my home country of Bangladesh without a job and living on the streets."

Amit smiled at Annette. "I will forever be indebted to Miss Annette."

Annette reached out and hugged Amit. "You're like the son I never had." She released her grip and patted his back.

Millie could see her friend was uncomfortable with the display of affection and quickly changed the subject.

She turned to Andy, who thrust a brightly wrapped package into her hand. "This is for you."

Annette stared at the gift. "For me?"

Millie nodded. "Happy birthday."

Annette set it on the counter and started to take the paper off. She turned the box over. "Tell me you didn't…"

"I didn't," Millie said. "Andy did."

"We both did," Andy corrected.

Annette pulled the hot pink handheld Taser from the box and inspected it. "Fifty thousand volts and fifteen foot reach." She nodded. "Impressive."

She looked at Andy. "Can I try it on you?" she teased.

Andy took a step back. He held up his hands. "No way! I suggest you track down Brody."

The group chuckled. Many of them remembered Andy's recent Taser demonstration…how Brody had jerked the gun from Andy's hand and then zapped him good.

Andy had fallen to the floor and when he gained his sense of feeling back, had wrapped his hands around Brody's throat.

It had been tense moments. Looking back it had been hilarious.

Annette opened several more gifts including a police whistle, a wooden rack to hold her cookbooks and some special spices she'd been looking for that someone had managed to find on one of the islands.

It was late by the time the party ended and the girls left the kitchen. Millie was whupped and discouraged. For once, she was at a loss in an investigation. Someone was going to get away with murder.

Millie was the last to get ready for bed. Ariana was already asleep by the time Millie crawled onto her cot and slid under the covers.

Sometime during the night, Millie's subconscious remembered something that had happened in the jungle.

She remembered the face she saw hiding in the bushes and realized she recognized the person, even with the face paint. Was it the face of a murderer?

It dawned on her why Kay and Pierre hadn't bothered to go after Ariana's fanny pack...because it wasn't them! It was Christopher and he didn't need the pack because he had seen the map when he and Ariana had searched for the evidence!

All he had left to do now was get rid of Ariana! That was probably what he was doing when she caught a glimpse of him in the jungle!

Millie awoke abruptly and bolted upright in bed. The first beams of daylight peeked through the edges of the curtain. A cold chill ran through Millie's body. Ariana's bed was empty.

Millie prayed that Ariana had stepped out on the balcony. She crawled out of bed, wandered over to the door and peeked through the glass. The balcony was empty.

Millie tapped on Kay's cabin door and Kay, who was still wearing yesterday's outfit, finally answered. "Is Ariana in there?"

Kay ran a hand through her hair. "No. I haven't seen her since last night. Why?"

"Because her life is in danger!"

***

Ariana crept out of bed, quickly changed her clothes in the bathroom and then stepped into the hall. She knew she should be able to trust Millie after all this time, but the ex-cop in her couldn't.

Christopher had asked her to meet him up in the VIP area where they could talk without anyone else around...namely Firkin or one of

Ariana's assistants. Christopher had told her they should not trust the two employees.

Ariana had to agree. Trust no one…including Millie.

The skies were still dark and there was a light chill in the air as Ariana stepped out onto the deck. No one was around, not even the cleaning crew as she climbed the few steps that led to the VIP area.

She could see Christopher's silhouette as he leaned over the rail and stared out at the dark water. He turned when Ariana approached.

The smell of cigarette smoke lingered in the air. It was a nasty habit and Ariana had tried to convince Christopher that he would feel much better if he quit. Christopher had argued he had few vices and planned to keep this indulgence.

"Did you bring it?" he asked when she got close.

Ariana nodded her head as she removed the fanny pack from her waist. "Yeah. You gonna call Gatwick?"

Christopher nodded. "He's waiting. As soon as the Miami skyline is in view, we should have cell phone reception."

Ariana carefully draped the pack on the rail between them.

Christopher took a deep drag off his cigarette and then tossed the butt over the rail. "What's your plan now that this assignment is over?"

Her skin began to crawl. For some reason, Christopher was starting to make her nervous.

Ariana slid her toe out of her sandal and tapped her bare foot on the teak deck. "I'm not sure." She shrugged. "Got a few things on the backburner," she added noncommittally.

"I'm sorry Ariana," Christopher softly whispered.

Ariana turned at the exact moment Christopher reached both hands forward and wrapped them around her throat.

***

Millie ran to the bathroom, threw on the first thing she could find – her outfit from the night before. She quickly brushed her teeth, washed her face and ran a comb through her hair before she slipped her shoes on, grabbed her lanyard and darted to the door.

Kay had already changed clothes and was waiting for Millie. "Who?"

"Christopher. The boyfriend." If that was even his name. Millie had a hunch Miguel had noticed something about Christopher or his passport and when confronted, Christopher killed him, making it look like Ariana had possibly done it, or someone who was with Ariana to throw the police off!

Millie darted across the back of the dark theater. Kay was right on her heels.

Millie picked up her radio and called Dave Patterson. "Patterson, do you copy?"

There was a momentary silence and Millie prayed he would answer. "Go ahead Millie."

"I need to talk to you. Stat."

"I'm in my office."

When Kay and Millie arrived, Patterson wasn't in his office. He was outside in the hallway pacing, his hands behind his back, a serious expression on his face.

"It's Spade. He's the killer," Patterson said as soon as Millie got close.

Millie frowned. "Who is Spade?"

"Lance Spade, posing as Christopher Johnson. We just got word from Miami PD they found

Christopher Johnson's body in a dumpster near the port. There was no ID on the body and it took a few days to figure out who he was."

Patterson eyed Kay but continued to talk. Millie was certain that he'd already had her checked out.

"Johnson was an ex special operative so it was hard to figure out who he was, something Lance Spade probably knew. He figured by the time authorities ID'd the body, he would be long gone with the map, and probably flying back to Chicago to blackmail Gatwick."

"Ariana would be dead, Johnson blamed and Spade long gone."

Millie stared past Dave Patterson's shoulder. This meant that if Lance Spade hadn't killed Ariana, he was close. The ship would be docking soon and her gut told her he planned to be one of the first off, leaving Ariana's body behind.

"Danielle Kneldon," Millie said.

It was Patterson's turn to be surprised. "Who is Danielle Kneldon?"

"Ariana Teliar aka Gatwick. The real one is in hiding. Danielle boarded the ship, posing as the young heiress, hired by Ariana's father."

"Why?"

Millie sighed. "It's a long story, but Spade doesn't know that. All he knows is Ariana is the only other person who knows where the lost Mayan civilization is."

She went on. "We need to start searching for Ariana."

"I hope she's still alive," Kay fretted.

Millie did, too. She still felt responsible for the young woman.

Patterson nodded. "We already have security staff searching every nook and cranny of the ship."

"Nothing yet?"

Patterson glumly shook his head. "No. It's almost as if they vanished."

Millie hoped Christopher…or whoever he was, hadn't thrown Ariana overboard.

Patterson's radio began to crackle. "Hey boss. I think we have something." Millie recognized the voice on the other end. It was Oscar, one of the security staff and Patterson's right hand man.

Patterson lifted the radio to his lips. "Whatcha got?"

"Meet me in the VIP deck area."

Millie's heart sank. The VIP area was located on the top deck of the ship. It was off the beaten path and somewhat secluded. It was the same spot where a few months back, one of the passengers had gone overboard.

Millie hoped they didn't have a second, similar casualty. Patterson voiced what Millie thought. "Is that spot cursed?"

The trio started for the top of the ship. When they arrived at the VIP, the area was crawling with security. Oscar was in the thick of the crowd.

He broke free when he saw Patterson. The first thing Millie noticed was that he was holding something.

Her blood froze when she realized it was Ariana's fanny pack.

Oscar handed it to Patterson. "We found this draped over the railing, along with a shoe." He pointed to one of the other security guards who held a woman's sandal. The pattern on top of the sandal was a beaded starfish.

It didn't look familiar to Millie. She turned to Kay, whose face was white as a ghost. Millie asked the question, but she already knew the answer. "That shoe…it belongs to Ariana, doesn't it?"

Kay nodded. "Yes. It was one of her favorite pairs."

Millie shuffled to the railing and peered over the side. The sun was just coming up and she could see Miami's skyline off in the distance. Her gaze dropped to the water.

Even if Christopher, or Lance Spade, had just pushed her over the side, the chances of finding Ariana's body, let alone alive, were slim to none.

Dave Patterson turned the bag over in his hand. "You searched the entire ship?"

"Yes, sir." Oscar confirmed.

Patterson's shoulders sagged. "We need to start on the paperwork," he sighed. "We also need to start another top to bottom search for Spade."

Millie watched as Patterson and the security staff shuffled off the upper deck and headed down the steps.

Kay started to follow and then realized Millie had not moved. "Aren't we going to go down with them? I'm sure they want a statement since we were the last to see her alive."

Millie shook her head. The wheels were spinning. Ariana...Danielle, was smart. Maybe it was wishful thinking on her part, or maybe it was a sixth sense, but she felt that Ariana was still on board and hopefully alive.

She turned to face the water. Security had searched top to bottom, every nook and cranny...or had they?

She turned her head and gazed at the doors that led to the Sky Chapel. A few weeks back, Pastor Evans, knowing Millie's penchant for mysteries and intrigue, had shown Millie a secret room in the front of the chapel. The secret room was directly behind the cross.

The evening before, when Ariana and Millie were in the chapel, Ariana had noticed the space behind the cross and mentioned it to Millie, who told her about the secret hideaway.

Millie wondered if the security staff knew about the spot.

"C'mon." Millie motioned Kay to follow her. They stepped through the sliding doors and into the dark sanctuary. She made her way down the center aisle and onto the platform.

Millie slipped through the small opening in the back and ran her hand along the wall as she searched for the secret door handle.

Her fingers touched the metal pull and Millie lifted it to the side. "Ariana. Are you in there?"

Millie slid the door the rest of the way open and Ariana flopped out of the small space. Her eyes were wide open as she stared at Millie, as if to say, "Millie! Look out!"

Chapter 21

Millie felt a jolt of electricity burn through her body. Her legs gave out and she collapsed on the floor. Kay stood over the top of her, an evil grin on her face. "I'll get back to you in a minute. First things first."

Kay reached over Millie's limp body, grabbed Ariana's dangling arm and jerked her out of the small hiding space. She dragged her to the front of the sanctuary and released her grip.

Millie was confused. Ariana was not fighting back. It was as if she had been...drugged.

Millie watched the scene unfold in horror, unable to move. Her body began to twitch from electric aftershocks.

Kay looked at Ariana and then at Millie. "You first."

She shoved the Taser in her back pocket. Next, she reached down and grabbed both of

Millie's hands as she started to drag her across the floor toward the door.

A chill ran through Millie's body as she realized that Kay planned to dump her overboard! She willed her body to move, to fight, but the effects of the stun gun had paralyzed her nerves and she was helpless.

Millie did the only thing she could think to do – pray. "Dear Lord. Please save me. Save us!" she cried out silently.

Kay had managed to drag her out into the deserted VIP area. When they reached the edge of the railing, Kay bent down and slipped one arm under Millie's legs and the other arm under her back.

She started to lift Millie when suddenly; a yelp of pain escaped her lips. Kay released her hold on Millie and fell against the railing before she slid to the floor.

Millie blinked rapidly, unable to grasp the fact that she had been mere seconds from death.

Dave Patterson stood next to Kay's still form, a small gun in his hand. He grinned when he saw Millie staring at him in disbelief. "Two can play that game."

He reached down and wrapped his arms around Millie's motionless body as a security guard grabbed one of Kay's arms and snapped a cuff in place. With the second cuff secure, the guard rolled her over.

Patterson's crew carried Kay down the stairs and out of sight.

Millie lay there for what seemed like forever. Sharp pokes that felt like a thousand needles stabbing her ran up and down her spine. She was getting her feeling back! She moved her fingers and then her toes.

It was several more minutes before Millie was able to sit upright and her tongue no longer felt as if someone had glued it to the roof of her mouth.

Ariana emerged from the chapel, leaning heavily on Oscar. He helped her to one of the lounge chairs. She placed her head against the back of the chair and faced Millie. "Are you okay?"

Millie slowly nodded. "Yeah. That was a close one," she admitted.

Millie turned to Patterson. "How did you know?"

"Kay made a mistake. When we got back to the office, we went over the surveillance video from the area and caught a glimpse of Christopher Johnson and Kay walking this way. Moments later, only Kay returned."

He went on. "When we saw the footage, we raced back up here."

Millie was stunned. "Kay zapped Christopher and then shoved his paralyzed body over the rail?"

What a hideous way to die. Alive and alert, yet unable to do anything to save yourself.

He nodded. "Just like she planned to do to you and Ariana. I mean Danielle."

"But I thought it was Christopher," Millie was confused.

Patterson crossed his arms and leaned against the rail. "My theory is that it was Christopher...and Kay. Their scheme was to have Ariana lead them to the ruins. After she had done that, they planned to get rid of her."

Danielle nodded. "I suspected all along it might be Kay but when I found out Christopher, I mean Lance Spade, was a fake, I guess I let my guard down."

"Me, too," Millie admitted, disappointed with herself. "What about Miguel and the fact that someone conked Kay on the head and ransacked the apartment?"

"We'll have to wait to talk to Kay, but my guess is that Spade killed Miguel and then Spade and Kay faked the attack and break in of Ariana's suite to throw us off."

Millie remembered how Kay had described someone that sounded eerily like Firkin, as the person who ransacked the suite and hit her on the head. "How and where does Firkin fit in?"

Danielle spoke. "I can answer that. Gatwick warned me about him when we first went over this assignment. Firkin is another rich investor who backs these ancient digs. He is a very wealthy man, although you'd never guess by looking at him."

Millie had almost full range of motion and got to her feet. She impulsively reached out and hugged Patterson. "Thank you for saving my...our lives."

Patterson returned the hug and Millie could've sworn he actually blushed.

Danielle climbed out of the lounge chair and hugged Patterson, too. "I don't know you from Adam, but thank you for saving my life, too."

Patterson returned the hug, a little longer than he hugged Millie and Millie gave Patterson a sly smile as she stared at Danielle's back.

The group headed down the steps and made their way across the deck. Moments later, the ship silently eased into port.

Millie was never so glad to see Miami in her life. It wasn't that she hadn't had fun with Ariana/Danielle, although parts of the adventure were not quite fun. She was more than ready to return to her normal life.

Danielle headed to her cabin to pack while Millie headed to Andy's office to check in. Now that Danielle was leaving, Millie was anxious to get back to her regular schedule. She glanced down at her grimy uniform and hoped she would have time to change into a fresh one.

Andy's office was ablaze with lights as Millie made her way inside. Andy smiled when he saw Millie approach. "You don't know how relieved I am to have you back," he said.

Millie eased into the seat across from him. "Not half as happy as I am," she argued.

"True," he had to admit. "Ariana was a handful."

"Danielle," Millie corrected.

"Who is Danielle?" Andy asked.

"Never mind. It's a long story. Someday I'll fill you in," she promised.

Andy slid Millie's schedule across the table. She slipped her glasses on and picked up the sheet of paper.

Andy's radio went off. "Andy, do you copy?

Millie recognized the voice. It was Donovan Sweeney, the ship's purser.

Andy picked the radio off the table and pressed the button. "I'm here."

"Can you meet me in Patterson's office?"

"Now?"

"Now," Donovan confirmed.

"10-4." Andy turned to Millie. "Can you start debarkation? I'll catch up with you."

Millie gave a mock salute. "Yes, sir."

She followed Andy out of the office and the two of them parted ways at the landing. Millie headed up to deck five for passenger debarkation while Andy headed down the stairs to security.

Millie wondered what Patterson wanted with Andy, but promptly forgot as soon as she saw the long line of guests waiting to get off the ship.

Andy returned within the hour and joined Millie as they told the guests goodbye. During a lull in crowds, Millie asked Andy what Donovan and Patterson wanted.

Andy shook his head. "You'll find out soon enough," he said mysteriously.

After the last passenger had "dinged" their key card and headed down the ramp, Millie let out a sigh of relief. She had missed breakfast and was starving. On top of that, her feet were beginning to ache. "I'm going to grab a bite to eat and then shower and change. These are yesterday's clothes."

"I was wondering what smelled," Andy teased.

Millie shot him a dark look and stomped off, although she wasn't angry, just happy...happy to have her life and routine back.

Millie wandered into Waves, and grabbed a tray and plate at the end of the buffet. She loaded her plate with bacon, scrambled eggs, home fries and wheat toast. She was even able to squeeze in a small scoop of fresh fruit.

She juggled the heaping plate of food and stopped for a cup of coffee before heading through the sliders to a small bistro table that faced the water.

The place was deserted. All of the previous guests were long gone and the new arrivals had not yet started to board.

Millie *thought* the outdoor dining area was deserted. She spied someone sitting off in the corner. The figure looked familiar. Wisps of long blonde hair whipped around in the light breeze.

Millie started to sit at a small table off to the side but curiosity got the better of her. She approached the woman. "Hello?"

The woman turned around. It was Danielle!

Millie nearly dumped her tray, right then and there! "W-what..."

Danielle grinned. "Surprised to see me?"

Surprised wasn't the word. Someone could have knocked Millie over with a feather. No, shock was a more accurate description.

"Why..."

"Why am I still here? I finished my assignment. All I have to do is make a quick trip to Fed Ex a small package to Gatwick and I'm a free agent so I stopped by Dave Patterson's office to find out if they needed any extra security crew."

Millie set her plate on the table and slumped into a nearby chair.

Danielle slid her plate to the side to make room for Millie's plate. "He said he'd check and called someone named Donovan who said they would have to check with Andy."

She shrugged. "I guess Andy said there was room for one more." She waved her hand in the air. "Voila! Looks like we will be co-workers. Isn't that great?"

The end. (Book 5, coming soon...)

Visit <u>hopecallaghan.com</u> for information on special offers and soon-to-be-released books!

If you enjoyed reading Deadly Deception, please take a moment to leave a review. It would be greatly appreciated! Thank you!

Pumpkin Pecan Cobbler

Ingredients
1 cup + 3 tablespoons all-purpose flour
2 teaspoons baking powder
½ teaspoon salt
¾ cup granulated sugar
1 teaspoon cinnamon
½ teaspoon nutmeg
½ cup pumpkin puree
¼ cup milk
¼ cup melted butter
1-1/2 teaspoons vanilla

Topping
½ cup granulated sugar
½ cup brown sugar
¼ cup chopped pecans
1-1/2 cups very hot water

Directions
Preheat oven to 350 degrees.

In a medium-sized bowl, blend flour, spices, baking powder, sugar and salt.

In a smaller bowl, mix pumpkin, melted butter, vanilla and milk. Once blended, pour this into dry ingredients (above). Mix well.

Pour mixed wet and dry ingredients into 8-inch casserole dish with high sides. (I used a glass pie dish & it worked great.)

In a separate bowl, mix <u>topping ingredients</u>: sugar (granulated sugar and brown sugar), and chopped pecans) until blended.

Spread these dry ingredients evenly over the top of the batter. Pour the hot water over the entire surface. (NOTE: DO **NOT** STIR!)

Bake for 40 minutes or until the middle sets. (TIP: Place a baking sheet under the dish in case it bubbles over.)

Cool 5 – 10 minutes. Serve with vanilla ice cream.

Yield: 8 servings

About The Author

Hope Callaghan is an author who loves to write Christian books, especially Christian Mystery and Cozy Mystery books. Born and raised in a small town in West Michigan, she now lives in Florida with her husband.

She is the proud mother of one daughter and a stepdaughter and stepson. When she's not doing the thing she loves best - writing books - she enjoys cooking, traveling and reading books.

Hope loves to connect with her readers!

Visit **HopeCallaghan.com** for information on special offers and soon-to-be-released books!

Email: hope@hopecallaghan.com

Facebook page:
http://www.facebook.com/hopecallaghanauthor

Other Books by Author, Hope Callaghan:

DECEPTION CHRISTIAN MYSTERY SERIES:

Waves of Deception: Samantha Rite Series Book 1
Winds of Deception: Samantha Rite Series Book 2
Tides of Deception: Samantha Rite Series Book 3

GARDEN GIRLS CHRISTIAN COZY MYSTERIES SERIES:

Who Murdered Mr. Malone? Book 1
Grandkids Gone Wild: Book 2
Smoky Mountain Mystery: Book 3
Death by Dumplings: Book 4
Eye Spy: Book 5
Magnolia Mansion Mysteries: Book 6
Missing Milt: Book 7
Bully in the 'Burbs: Book 8
Garden Girls Christian Cozy Mysteries Boxed Set Books 1-4

CRUISE SHIP CHRISTIAN COZY MYSTERIES SERIES:

Starboard Secrets Cruise Ship Cozy Mysteries Book 1
Portside Peril: Cruise Ship Cozy Mysteries Book 2
Lethal Lobster: Cruise Ship Cozy Mysteries Book 3

Made in the USA
Columbia, SC
23 May 2025